CATCH ME

(A Katie Winter FBI Suspense Thriller—Book 10)

Molly Black

Molly Black

Bestselling author Molly Black is author of the MAYA GRAY FBI suspense thriller series, comprising nine books (and counting); of the RYLIE WOLF FBI suspense thriller series, comprising six books (and counting); of the TAYLOR SAGE FBI suspense thriller series, comprising eight books (and counting); of the KATIE WINTER FBI suspense thriller series, comprising eleven books (and counting); and of the RUBY HUNTER FBI suspense thriller series, comprising three books (and counting).

An avid reader and lifelong fan of the mystery and thriller genres, Molly loves to hear from you, so please feel free to visit www.mollyblackauthor.com to learn more and stay in touch.

ISBN: 978-1-0943-3030-3

BOOKS BY MOLLY BLACK

MAYA GRAY MYSTERY SERIES
GIRL ONE: MURDER (Book #1)
GIRL TWO: TAKEN (Book #2)
GIRL THREE: TRAPPED (Book #3)
GIRL FOUR: LURED (Book #4)
GIRL FIVE: BOUND (Book #5)
GIRL SIX: FORSAKEN (Book #6)
GIRL SEVEN: CRAVED (Book #7)
GIRL EIGHT: HUNTED (Book #8)
GIRL NINE: GONE (Book #9)

RYLIE WOLF FBI SUSPENSE THRILLER
FOUND YOU (Book #1)
CAUGHT YOU (Book #2)
SEE YOU (Book #3)
WANT YOU (Book #4)
TAKE YOU (Book #5)
DARE YOU (Book #6)

TAYLOR SAGE FBI SUSPENSE THRILLER
DON'T LOOK (Book #1)
DON'T BREATHE (Book #2)
DON'T RUN (Book #3)
DON'T FLINCH (Book #4)
DON'T REMEMBER (Book #5)
DON'T TELL (Book #6)
DON'T HIDE (Book #7)
DON'T BLINK (Book #8)

KATIE WINTER FBI SUSPENSE THRILLER
SAVE ME (Book #1)
REACH ME (Book #2)
HIDE ME (Book #3)
BELIEVE ME (Book #4)
HELP ME (Book #5)
FORGET ME (Book #6)
HOLD ME (Book #7)

PROTECT ME (Book #8)
REMEMBER ME (Book #9)
CATCH ME (Book #10)
WATCH ME (Book #11)

RUBY HUNTER FBI SUSPENSE THRILLER
IF I RUN (Book #1)
IF I TELL (Book #2)
IF I LIVE (Book #3)

PROLOGUE

Aaron West fastened the harnesses, his fingers numb in the sub-zero temperature, the barks from his team of Siberian huskies loud and excited in the icy morning. The cold wind prickled his spine, strangely chilling. Although Aaron loved the thrill of racing, he wasn't used to the temperatures this far north. He found these early morning exercise sessions cold and lonely, even though they were necessary to acclimatize him and the dogs to the race conditions and terrain.

Over the past few days, as he and his dogs had sped across the snow, it had made him realize what a desolate area they were inhabiting as they prepared for the annual Sled Dog Festival in Soaring Crow, far north in Yukon territory, Canada. Going out alone in this remote area gave him a strange, chilling sense of isolation he'd never had before.

In a way, Aaron found these vast, silent landscapes creepy. Where he trained at home, in northern Minnesota, there were always signs of civilization around. Not here, and it made him wonder - what would happen if the worst occurred during an exercise session? Who would find him if he fell from the sled and the thick, falling snow covered his tracks?

And at the same time, for no logical reason at all, he'd had a tingling feeling yesterday that he was being watched, that there were eyes out there, looking. Just not ones he could see.

Pushing his dark hair back, tucking it under his fur hat, Aaron tried to push the thoughts aside as well. He had no idea why he was feeling so paranoid, and put it down to pre-race pressure. As one of the top favorites for the sprint section of the racing festival, he had to do his best and try to bring the trophy home for the USA.

The dogs knew for sure that there was a race to run. His team of sixteen dogs loved to run, and they loved the snow. He was exercising them in two teams of eight, so this team would be his first time out today. With a rest day yesterday, the dogs were full of energy, leaping and yelping as he slipped the harnesses onto their thick, soft, fur coats that were double-layer, and therefore superbly insulated against the cold.

This was his naughtiest team; these dogs were the reserves. His core team of eight fully trained dogs would exercise next. But his first run, with these younger, more willful dogs, was always a handful.

Tess, his youngest husky, was being a particular challenge today. Exuberant and naughty, in another year, she would be a great runner, and he thought that she had all the makings of a lead dog – fast and intelligent, able to set the pace and show the team the way. She wasn't going to be large or strong enough to be a wheel dog – these were the dogs at the back of the sled, whose power helped pull the sled around corners, trees, and other hazards. For the time being, she was a team dog, in the middle of the pack, until she'd learned the ropes.

But she was always one to take advantage. As his chilled fingers battled with the fastenings, Tess slipped away, escaping the harness. She set off across the snow on her own, racing out into the wilderness for the sheer joy of it.

"Tess! Tess!" Aaron called in exasperation.

She didn't listen, of course. Deaf to his cries and whistles. The naughtiest dog in his pack for sure. Sled dogs had to be smart and responsive, and when in harness, she reacted immediately to his voice commands. But when she was not in harness – well, then, not so much.

After making sure the other dogs were all secure and couldn't follow her, he put on his snowshoes and set off after her, trudging out across the snow. This wasn't the route he'd intended to take. He was going to head out across the ice on a fast, smooth route that led through the pine forest, dark in the distance, and out into the icy wasteland beyond where the wind blew relentlessly.

But Tess had veered to the side and run into a craggier section of terrain, which hopefully meant it would slow her down because this dog was a speed queen when she got going.

As Aaron slipped and stumbled after her in the deep, uneven snow, he saw that this section of terrain was more broken, with slopes and rocky outcrops.

If he lost her, he could waste valuable time hunting for her.

The wind whipped at his face, nipping at his cheeks. He pushed his hat down lower, trying to protect his skin. His eyes narrowed, fighting the glare.

He shouted again in exasperation, "Tess!"

Sometimes the life of a dog musher was more cold and frustration than glamour and excitement, he acknowledged, slipping on an icy rock half-hidden in the snow. His breath clouded in the cold.

Behind him, the low buildings of the encampment where he, his dogs, and a few other teams were staying, already seemed far in the distance.

But there she was! She hadn't gone too far, he saw with a rush of relief. She could easily be over the horizon by now if she'd had that idea in mind, but it seemed that something closer to home had fascinated the wayward husky.

She was nose-deep in the snow, digging energetically with her front paws.

Aaron grasped the leash, ready to attach it to the harness. With his other hand, he dug in his pocket for a treat, something to lure her closer.

But she seemed oblivious to him as she dug, snow spraying in all directions.

And then, she did something weird, something he'd never seen her do before.

She backed away a couple of steps from the place she'd been digging and she let out a high pitched, unearthly howl.

The sound was so intense, so unexpected, that it chilled his blood.

"Tess, what's up? Are you hurt?" he asked, scrambling over the snow, feeling a massive sense of relief as the leash clipped into the harness and he had her safe again.

Quickly, he checked her over, but she didn't seem injured. She seemed distracted, though, looking and pulling toward that disturbed place in the snow.

Aaron frowned, intrigued. "What is it, Tess?"

She growled, a low, threatening sound, almost as if she didn't like him approaching that place. All the hairs on his skin stood up in warning. Slowly, he reached out and brushed the snow away from the shallow indentation she'd made.

And he cried aloud.

A sheet-white face stared back at him. The mound of snow, he now saw, was a partially covered body, its hands outflung, snow piled over the thick winter clothing.

He stared down, gripping the leash, his breath coming fast as adrenaline flooded him.

3

This was no accident. That, he saw immediately.

The body was undisturbed apart from one large and clearly fatal wound.

The bloody slash across this man's neck, now frozen red, told Aaron that something - or more likely, someone - had intentionally killed this victim. Such a clean wound, no sign of mauling - an animal could surely not have done this, he decided with a chill.

With a sense of mounting horror, he realized he was staring down at a murder scene.

CHAPTER ONE

"What can we do?" FBI agent Katie Winter asked the doctor, her voice tense, her fingers tugging at her thick brown hair. "What can we do for Josie?"

They were in a side room in the Rochester General Hospital where her twin, Josie, was now in the third week of her stay after Katie had rescued her.

Katie couldn't bear to think what Josie must have endured in the years since her abduction, after a kayaking accident, at the age of sixteen. She'd spent that long again - sixteen years - in the clutches of the evil and insane Gabriel Rath, who had hidden her away.

Finally, Katie had realized where she was and tracked him down to his cabin deep in the wilderness. In a confrontation with the mentally damaged man that had turned violent, Katie had ended up killing him accidentally. He'd jumped into the path of the shot she'd fired at his knife arm to save herself. Those moments were something which still haunted her nightmares.

But the damage Josie had suffered was deeper and more serious than they had first thought.

Her body was healing well from its state of near starvation. She was clean and cared for, her skin was clear, she was putting on weight, her teeth had been seen to - under sedation - and her hair washed and trimmed - also under sedation.

Because when Josie was not under sedation, she was in a semi-catatonic state, and the only interruptions to it happened when she surged awake into terrified violence.

Not once had Katie seen any flash of recognition in her twin's wide green eyes. She didn't know Katie, she didn't even seem to understand the hospital environment. She'd mostly forgotten how to speak, uttering grunts and shrill, animal-like cries.

The staff at the hospital had been patient and compassionate, but the team was at a loss as to how to help her. Katie had visited every day, staying by Josie's bedside, as had her parents. She had tried to talk to her, tried to touch her, tried to arouse some response, but she'd been largely unsuccessful. All she seemed to trigger was a violent need to attack.

Katie was determined to find a way to help her twin. She hadn't given up when Josie had been abducted, and she wouldn't give up now. She wouldn't leave her sister until she was back to the way she used to be. It was her new, burning goal in life to see her return to normal, to see peace and life back in her face, instead of terror and desperation.

"We're doing what we can, Agent Winter," the doctor said quietly. "We're doing what we can. But we can't force her to get better. So far, we've tried every therapy and intervention that normally works in such circumstances. But none of them have made a difference, and the psychiatrist in charge of her recovery actually feels that she's regressed in the past week."

Those words chilled Katie. Standing in the small, brightly lit room, next to a metal trolley stacked with equipment and two chairs, she felt as if she was hearing a verdict of doom.

"Regressed?" she asked, anxiety flaring.

"Yes. He's been monitoring certain important progress markers. She should be achieving these regularly, exceeding them, and reaching new markers. But she's been failing to achieve certain milestones that were in place a week ago."

"Such as?"

"Eating solid food. There's no reason for it. Nothing wrong health wise, and her teeth are fine now, but she won't accept it. She'll only sip on liquids, so we're back to soups and purees. And she has stopped being able to go to the bathroom on her own again. She - when left to herself, she squats in the corner of the room."

"Oh, no," Katie said, feeling a frisson of dread.

"These are important, basic milestones. That's not even taking into account the resistance and fear she's showing to the nurses. When she's in a catatonic state, she can at least be managed. But when she isn't, when she's in a manic state, she's unmanageable. So we're having to increase her sedation."

Katie felt horrified by this. What was the answer, she agonized. Were there going to be any answers?

"What's the next step?" she asked, her mouth dry.

The doctor ran a hand through his short, dark brown hair, his lean face worried and serious above his scrubs.

"The psychiatric team has suggested electroconvulsive therapy," the doctor said.

Katie gasped. "But that - I mean, I don't know much about it. But I do know it has some bad side effects? There's no going back from them, either?"

He nodded grimly. "Undoubtedly, ECT is a treatment of last resort. But it has had good success in treating schizophrenia and intense mania. The most common side effect is memory loss, and yes, as you say, that can be permanent. And it can cause brain damage, too. But at this stage, it looks like we are speeding toward a worst-case scenario without it."

Katie took a deep, shaky breath. This was so bad. It was worse than she'd ever imagined. It was as if her sister's predicament had turned into a nightmare that was worsening, trapping her in twists and turns of a doom-laden prognosis.

"I guess if we have to, we must, but - I'd still like some time to think about it. And to speak to my parents about it. It - it feels so final. So extreme. Is there nothing else we can try?"

The doctor said softly, "I'm sorry, Katie. I know this is hard. We are extremely worried and disappointed. It's unheard of that a patient doesn't improve, and is regressing, on the therapies and drugs we've tried so far. Time is running out; the doctors here have all the information on her decline. I'm going to give you these papers. They outline what she's gone through medically, and the state of her body and health. They also explain how we feel we need to treat her more aggressively, and why it's now urgent." He handed her a folder.

"What about a new medication?" she asked desperately. "Has the psychiatrist tried anything that's new on the market? Aren't they coming up with better drugs to treat this kind of problem?"

"For people who have responded mentally to a situation the way your sister has, it's unfortunate that treatment options are limited. The mind is a very complex thing, and it's often beyond the powers of drugs to fight against the damage that must have been done during those years."

Katie felt guilt flood her again. She had caused this. It had been her suggestion to go kayaking when the river was in flood. Josie's canoe had capsized thanks to her. She'd been abducted as a direct result of Katie's irresponsible decision.

She forced her attention back to the doctor.

"That's what we have been trying. A new drug on the market. But it's not having the effects we hoped. The only other option is to increase the dosage which will really be equivalent to using it off-label, as she's already on maximum dosage. And other than this, we're all out of options. We have tried everything. The ECT that I've just mentioned to you is the last chance we have."

Katie was aware of a feeling of panic building within her, and she felt sick. She wanted to run away, to hide from the situation, to fight against the bad news. She wanted to wake up, to open her eyes and find out that it was all a dream.

She wanted to escape from this reality, from this nightmare. But she couldn't. She had to live through it. And somehow, she had to find a way to help her twin.

"All right," she said at last, knowing that she had to face up to it. "I'll speak to my parents right now, and we'll go from there."

She turned away, knowing that this conversation would be tough, and that her parents would be as traumatized about this decision as she herself was. Would they want to agree to damaging Josie's brain and memory, in exchange for trying to conquer the demons that now inhabited her mind?

Feeling discouraged and as if the last shred of hope had gone, Katie turned and walked out of the hospital room, preparing herself for the difficult confrontation ahead.

CHAPTER TWO

Katie walked out of the hospital and crossed the road, feeling utterly traumatized by the decision confronting her. She didn't want to subject her twin to what she perceived to be a brutal, dangerous mode of therapy. But her parents also needed to weigh up the pros and cons of this treatment.

She realized that the morning traffic was getting heavier as she headed for the small guesthouse nearby that had become her parents' second home, where they had spent more time recently than at their real home, an hour and a half's drive away.

Walking into the guesthouse, she headed straight for their upstairs suite which consisted of a cozy bedroom and a small living room. She could smell the aroma of coffee, and hear the clink of cutlery from the dining room as breakfast got under way.

Tapping on the door, she waited to hear her parents' voices. Sure enough, her mother opened it a moment later.

"Katie. How's Josie this morning?"

Katie shook her head, feeling a sudden wave of emotion. This ordeal had taken its toll on all of them.

Already, after years of believing Josie dead, the pressure had its effects on her parents. Her father's hair was graying, his face grim, his once-ready smile now a rare occurrence. Her mother, always slim, was now too thin, her face haggard, lined with worry and grief.

Now, with Josie's current situation, her parents looked no better and she could see the stress was wearing them away.

In a way, her parents still felt like strangers to her after their long estrangement, even though they'd spent time together in the past few weeks. Katie was realizing the damage done to their relationship would also not heal fast. It was something that might never recover. After all, they had been living completely separate lives for sixteen years. Ever since Josie had disappeared, and they'd ended up blaming Katie in their grief, Katie hadn't felt she'd had parents at all.

"No change in Josie's condition," Katie said quietly. "In fact, there's bad news."

She looked around the small living room, where her mother stood anxiously at the door and her father sat on the plaid couch.

"Bad news?" her mother asked, her voice high.

"She's regressing. She's not achieving progress markers that she achieved a week ago."

Her mother pressed her lips together and Katie saw tears in her eyes.

"I've been suspecting so. From the way she's been reacting and what the nurses have been saying, I've been fearing it," she said quietly.

"I'm really sorry to tell you this, but the doctors want Josie to have ECT, or electroconvulsive therapy. As a matter of urgency. They've tried everything else, and they are very concerned about her decline."

"ECT?" her father said, sounding worried. "Are you talking about the electric shock treatment? Is that what they are recommending? It's dangerous, isn't it?"

"ECT is a high-risk procedure," her mother added in a shaky voice. "I don't think we can do that to Josie. What if it does permanent damage? Oh, no."

"Look, Mom, Dad, let me explain," Katie said, suddenly aware how upset her parents were. "It's serious. We're at a breaking point here. The doctors think that ECT is the last thing they can do. They say they've tried everything and Josie is just not responding."

"But that? Sending an electric current through the brain to produce a seizure? She's so traumatized already, I don't know how that can help. What if it makes her worse?"

"She's already not getting better," Katie reminded her.

Her mother sighed.

"We need some time to think about this. It's so traumatic. I know it's wrong of me to think this, but in a way, I wish you'd never found her, that she'd passed away. At least she'd be out of her suffering then."

"Mom!" Katie said, shocked. "How can you say such a thing?"

"Easily," her mother said, looking at Katie, and for a moment she seemed to be a stranger rather than a parent.

"That's not something I thought I'd hear you say," her father added, his tone accusing as he stared at his wife. "You're basically saying you would rather she suffered and died?"

"She's suffering now! Suffering terribly! And so are we! I just don't see a way out of this! It feels like we're all caught in a worst case scenario!"

"I know," Katie said. She felt utterly discouraged. It seemed like the brief, tenuous healing in their relationship had been broken and destroyed, and now her parents were fighting with each other as well.

Her finding Josie hadn't helped any of them; it had only made the stress worse. At least Josie was now warm, fed, and safe - but her mother was right. She was still suffering. Her demons were lodged in her mind and there seemed no escape.

What a terrible situation, and with no hope on the horizon and only the prospect of a therapy that might destroy her twin's mind completely.

"We have some time to think about it and talk about it, but not much," she said sadly.

Katie's hopes had never felt more futile. Self-blame filled her again. This was her doing. All of this. This friction, conflict, misery, and lives destroyed. All due to her one irresponsible action. How could she ever atone for this? She had tried; she'd felt as if she was fighting every step of the way with Josie, to get her back to normal.

And she'd gotten nowhere.

At that moment, her phone started ringing.

It was her boss, Detective Scott, calling, and seeing his name on the screen reminded Katie with a jolt that she was juggling work and family life. Recently, her sister's predicament had taken priority to the extent she'd taken two weeks' leave from the cross-border task force she was part of.

Scott had been sympathetic and understanding, but ultimately, Katie was a member of an elite crime fighting force and she knew she could not stay by this hospital bed indefinitely. There would come a time when she'd have to leave and get back to the important responsibilities of her work. That time might be now. She never thought this would take so long. She'd assumed that in two weeks, Josie's recovery would be almost complete.

"I'd better take this. It's my boss," she said tonelessly, but it was as if her parents hadn't even heard.

Katie walked out of the room, feeling as if she was suffering from an overdose of stress, exhaustion, and emotions.

"Detective Scott," she said.

"Katie. How's your sister?" he asked.

"Not great. She's not improving," Katie said flatly.

Scott sighed. "That's unfortunate. I'm so sorry to hear it." He paused. "There's an urgent case that I need you on. I'm afraid that you may have to leave her side for a short while at least."

Katie took a breath. "Leave? Now?" Panic flared. Now was a terrible time, with so many important decisions to make about her sister.

But Scott continued, sounding adamant. "There's nobody else who can take this on. The rest of the team are investigating a multiple murder case in North Dakota. The perpetrators have fled into Saskatchewan. Leblanc can't be on his own here. It's a very serious and potentially difficult situation. Very complex, because it involves an international event. So I need you on it. I'm sorry, Katie. I've given you all the time you can take." Scott's voice was firm.

"I understand," she said quietly, now realizing that the consequences of her actions could not extend to destroying her career, as well as her family. She would have to go, turn her back on Josie for a while. She needed to support her investigation partner Leblanc. He deserved nothing less.

"I'm sending the details through now. Take a look. And I'm going to have to get you on a flight, far north. In fact, I think I'll send Leblanc to join you in New York and charter you both a flight from there. This is a very urgent, very troubling case." Scott paused. "You are my best investigator, Katie. I wouldn't want it in any other hands. This needs to be solved, before it blows up in all of our faces."

He cut the call.

A moment later, Katie's phone beeped and she opened it, reading with growing intrigue about the latest, challenging case.

CHAPTER THREE

Three hours later, with her small travel bag packed, Katie was standing in Rochester International Airport, waiting for Leblanc to arrive so they could board their charter flight. It was going to take them deep into the northern part of the Yukon, to a scene where two brutal, bloody, and inexplicable murders had occurred in the last two days.

The Sled Dog Festival, in Soaring Crow, Yukon Territory, was an annual event that was pivotal to tourism in this northerly area, and the entire town of Soaring Crow had created an industry out of it - with the month-long festival consisting of different lengths of sled races, as well as other winter sports, hiking, skiing, and more.

The town, during summer, was a training ground for dry-land sledding, and a location for several top breeders of sled dogs, ranging from Siberian huskies to Alaskan Malamutes.

It was very clear to Katie, reading the background on the case, that Soaring Crow survived and thrived as a result of this massive international event that brought contestants and visitors from over twenty countries together.

Right now, the crowds were gathered at Soaring Crow - and killings were already putting this festival in jeopardy.

At that moment, Katie looked up to see Detective Leblanc approaching.

His normally stern, handsome, olive-skinned features lit up when he saw her and his dark eyes sparkled. She stared at him, feeling a mixture of happiness and regret.

Happiness, because she was with him again, out on a case, in his company, working with the synergy that had characterized a relationship that had started out with friction and conflict.

But regret, because the trauma with Josie had convinced Katie she was not yet ready or capable for an emotional relationship. She'd called off her budding romance with Leblanc, and although he'd accepted it and respected her predicament, Katie couldn't help a feeling of deep conflict. She was unsure if it had been the right choice. But for her own emotional sake, she wanted to shut things down - for now, anyway.

It had been more than two weeks since she'd seen Leblanc, and she saw he had a fresh haircut in that time, the precise angles bringing out his strong features. And she didn't recognize the warm, navy jacket he was wearing which looked to be new.

"Katie," he said, smiling.

"Leblanc. It's good to see you."

"The news on Josie is not good?" He'd received the brief text updates she'd sent.

Katie shook her head.

"I'm sorry," Leblanc said. "I hope there is a solution to be found."

"Me, too," she agreed. She didn't want to speak about it now, but appreciated that he'd asked, and shown sympathy.

Quickly, they went through passport control - a formality, since their passports were endorsed for cross-border travel without needing this step - and then they hurried out of the airport and over to the small plane that was waiting to take them far north.

Katie greeted the pilot, took her seat, fastened her seatbelt, and opened her laptop, immersing herself again in the details of the case.

Two victims had died so far and the modus operandi had been the same in both instances.

The coroner had deduced that the victims had been knocked out by a hard blow to the head, and then dragged, or carried, to the killing sites. There, their throats had been slashed by a deep, strong, and purposeful cut.

"A sharp blade was used, and there were no hesitation marks on either victim," the coroner had noted.

The first victim was Thomas Briggs, a local businessman and fifty-year-old notary who dealt with property sales in town. The other was Kevin Matthews, a twenty-eight-year old visitor from out of town, who attended the festival annually and set up a kiosk selling dog collars, equipment, harnesses, and other items that the racers needed.

There seemed to be no connection between them. Kevin had been found dumped in the snow a couple of hundred yards from his kiosk. A group of hikers had literally stumbled over his body yesterday afternoon. And then, this morning, one of the racers had found Thomas's body, after his dog had run away and dug in the snow that had covered it.

14

The RCMP were already swarming to the festival from other areas in Yukon Territory to offer more security and visible policing to the guests and travelers.

But Katie knew that if they were up against a serial killer, it would take more than a few more officers to deter this person from killing again.

She sighed. This case looked deeply troubling, and the potential for catastrophe was huge. This could, indeed, impact heavily on the tourism that was the heart and soul of this town.

The fact there were so many tourists in one small area, all virtual strangers to each other and from all over the globe, would make it even more complicated, because local knowledge was often an important contributor to solving these crimes.

"What do you think of this?" she asked Leblanc.

"I see no connection between these two victims," he said, his face serious. "That bothers me. I want to know how he is picking them. Is it random, that they were in the wrong place at wrong time? Or is there a deeper motive we haven't yet discovered?"

"We need to look for hidden links," Katie agreed.

"I hope, when we arrive, the site itself gives us a clue," Leblanc said. "Perhaps we will realize something that is not obvious from these notes and early reports."

As the plane headed north, Katie stared out of the window, watching the faraway territory scroll by, slowly changing from spring green, to the icier and more desolate tracts of land which were still in late winter's grip.

She hoped that among this inhospitable terrain, they could find where this killer was hiding, and stop his deadly agenda.

Hopefully, before he killed again.

*

Three hours later, the plane touched down on a private runway in a very different setting. The small aircraft jolted over the uneven runway, braking sharply just before the mound of packed snow that signaled its end.

Turning, the pilot taxied back until they were closer to the warehouse-like building that was the airport and hangar. Katie and

Leblanc got out of the plane, squeezing their way between the crates of supplies in the hold.

It was cold, and they both fastened their jackets tightly, stamping their feet and rubbing their hands, grabbing gloves and scarves from their carry-ons as they collected their bags and thanked the pilot, who was going to go on to another drop-site before transporting some goods back down to Toronto.

Katie saw one of the RCMP officers from Yukon Territory waiting for them near the hangar door.

"Agent Winter and Detective Leblanc," she said, striding forward to make introductions.

The officer, who had cherry-red cheeks and a shock of dark, curly hair, also looked cold, but he gave them a warm and friendly nod of greeting.

"I'm Officer Franc. I'm glad you're here. I've been policing this event for years, and nothing like this has ever happened. Everyone's in a state of complete shock, and panicking. This festival is such a high point for the town, and usually the worst that happens is a sled overturning, or someone slipping on the ice on the way back from the bar."

"I hope we can find out who's been doing this," Katie agreed.

"Where do you want to go first? I've brought along an SUV you're welcome to use. Just drop me back at the RCMP headquarters when you're ready."

Katie exchanged a glance with Leblanc.

"I think our first stop should be the witness who found the second body," Leblanc suggested. "A man on his own, and a race competitor - we could find out if he heard or saw anything. Perhaps you can take us there, and we can also view the scene before we drop you off."

"I can do that. His name's Aaron West, and he's accommodated in our Polaris cabin. We named all the accommodation after stars. Part of the tourism effort. He's expecting to be interviewed, so let's make a start there."

The agreeable but worried RCMP officer climbed into the car, with Katie and Leblanc stowing their bags and then piling in. The cold was biting, and the wind was sending snow flurrying into the air. It really was freezing here, and the difference in temperature reminded Katie how far north they were, and how different and remote this area was.

She wondered if the killer had traveled here, using this race, and the change in environment, as a springboard to start living his deadly fantasies.

But she also knew that if they were going to shine the spotlight on visitors, there would be literally hundreds of suspects. There were the dog handlers, the sledders or 'mushers,' there were tourists and supporters, judges and officials, friends and relatives. As the car drove through the town, she could see how busy it looked. Pubs and restaurants had lights in the windows and were doing a brisk lunchtime trade. Cars were parked all along Main Street, with number plates that showed some people had driven here from other parts of Canada, from Alaska, and even the northern USA states.

This festival was big business, and Katie knew that from here on, the pressure to solve this case fast would be immense.

"Here we are. This is the Polaris cabin," the officer said. They'd driven out of town now, and into the demarcated area of the large festival grounds that seemed to cover many acres. Here, he'd veered to the left, heading for the more remote residential buildings that had large dog runs and accommodations attached, as well as space for sleds and a host of paraphernalia.

Katie climbed out, feeling eager to meet the witness who had discovered the second body, while out on his own. His testimony, and a look at the scene, would give her a strong starting point and ground her in this case. There might even be some evidence she could find on the scene that would link to the killer.

Or so, at least, she hoped.

CHAPTER FOUR

Katie and Leblanc climbed out of the SUV outside the Polaris building and approached the lodgings with Officer Franc walking behind them. The name sounded grander than the place itself, which was a humble looking wooden cabin with a sloping roof and what looked to be thickly insulated walls. It was set among a snow-covered garden of shrubs, and behind the building Katie could see a covered dog run, from which volleys of excited barking could be heard.

They knocked on the door, and a moment later it was opened by a tall, fit-looking man wearing a green parka. His dark hair was tied back in a short ponytail. His face looked weathered, and Katie guessed him to be in his mid-thirties, a little older than her. He exuded an air of energy and motivation. In every inch of his lean frame, Katie sensed this was a man who lived his passion. Who lived to race.

"We're from the investigation unit," she said briefly. "Are you Aaron West?"

"Yes, I am," he said.

"We need to ask you some questions, and also take a look at the scene where you found the body."

He pressed his lips together, as if not relishing this unpleasant task, but knowing it had to be done. "It's about a ten-minute walk from here. Shall we go now, and I can fill you in as we walk?" he asked.

"Sure," Katie said, with a brief glance at Leblanc and Officer Franc to make sure they were in agreement.

They headed outside, and Katie immediately pulled her jacket tighter. It was seriously cold on this side. The cabin had provided some shelter from the prevailing wind, which now ripped through her clothing, despite the cold weather gear she was wearing.

"Tell me what happened," she asked.

"I've been here a week, training. I took my first team of dogs out early this morning. A young dog escaped, and I went after her. She ran up this way. I don't know if it was by chance, or whether she smelled something. It had snowed the night before. She started digging in the

18

snow and - well, when I got there, I saw what she'd found. He was lying face up; you could see the injury immediately, although his body was frozen. It was a very shocking sight."

Katie remembered from reading the coroner's report, that this victim had most likely been dead for twelve hours at least, by the time he was found. So he would have been killed the previous night.

According to the coroner, the victims also had head injuries. However both had died from loss of blood, though.

That made Katie wonder if Briggs had been knocked out, transported somewhere while unconscious, and then killed when he was lying in the snow.

That would mean the killer had placed the bodies in these locations for a reason. And since the locations were both fairly close to where people lived, worked, and drove - perhaps the reason was so that they could be found.

If this killer had wanted to hide the bodies without a trace he could certainly have done so, in a far more remote part of Soaring Crow and its icy surroundings.

"Did you know the victim, Mr. Thomas Briggs?" Leblanc asked the racer.

"No, not at all. I'd never seen him before. I actually assumed, for one small moment, that maybe he was a hiker who'd been attacked by a bear, something like that."

"And why did you change your mind?" Katie questioned.

"Because I realized - well, it was only the one cut I could see. It didn't look like tooth or claw marks; it looked like a sharp blade had been used. To me, anyway."

"And then what did you do?"

"I called the police, immediately. From where I was standing. I moved away some, in case I disturbed anything. And I waited until they came, which was about ten minutes later, as there were police in town. Then I took my dog back. They interviewed me, and when we were done, I headed out with the dogs."

"You did?" Leblanc questioned, raising his eyebrows.

Aaron shrugged apologetically. "Sir, it's a big race. We have to train. I must say, though, I felt jumpy. Yesterday and today. I've been on the lookout for anything."

"Your movements yesterday afternoon?" Katie said, needing to clear him completely.

"Yesterday was a rest day for the dogs. I spent the day cleaning the harnesses, doing some preparation. And then from five p.m. I hit the gym. I have to be fit, too. I worked out for two hours and then spent some time in the sauna. Then I went straight to dinner with a couple of the other U.S. team members."

That cleared Aaron without a doubt, Katie realized. There would have been no time for him to have committed this crime. He had found the body, close to his lodgings, but he was not the perpetrator. Aaron was a very fit man, an experienced outdoorsman. He had gone out looking for a dog who had escaped, and then found a man who had been killed.

"Did you see anything that could be relevant?" she asked him. "Anything unusual? When you came home last night?"

He shook his head. "It was dark and snowing. I checked the dogs and fed them. That's a nonstop job at this time, because they need lots of feeding when they're training hard for a race. They can eat five times as much as a normal dog."

Katie nodded, understanding the level of care and attention this must take. No wonder Aaron hadn't had time to notice anything else.

"Then I went inside and got a fire going," he said.

"Did you have any interaction with the other victim, Kevin Matthews?" she asked.

"Not since I've been here. I did some business with him last year. He seemed like a really good guy. Very much a drifter, a traveler type. He'd choose a few locations, find out what they needed, arrive there, and set up shop. That was what he did, in various places, throughout the year. An interesting guy."

That indicated Kevin had no ties to the area. Their only lead in terms of personal connections would be the other victim, the local man, Thomas Briggs.

Katie looked at the area where they had arrived. It really was desolate, with rough, uneven ground, covered in ice and snow. And it was at least a hundred yards from the nearest road, she judged. So someone must have pulled, or carried, the body here. Why? Why had it been dumped here, close to a racer's lodgings, miles from anywhere?

And even though it had clearly been intended to be found, Katie also read that there had been no trace evidence at the scene. Looking at it now, she realized the futility of searching further. The body could have been dragged from a number of different directions, and last night's snowfall had effectively covered the tracks.

This was frustratingly short on evidence.

They turned and walked back, picking their way carefully through the deep, uneven snow.

"I think we should go and interview Thomas's family," Leblanc suggested. "As the victim who lived locally, perhaps he was aware of some trouble, something not right, a problem in the area. And perhaps he told people. He might have said something that could take us further."

"From the case notes, I remember he has a sister who lives in town, and also a father in the area?" Katie said.

"That's correct," Officer Franc agreed. "He's listed as divorced, from a few years ago, and I think she moved away."

"I agree that we need to speak to his family," Katie said. "I think it's important to go there. But before we do, there's one stop I want to make."

"Which is?" Leblanc asked.

"It's the race organizer's office. I want to find out exactly what this race involves, how long people have been here, if everyone who arrives here is correctly documented, and if they do background checks on any of the temporary staff."

"All good questions," Leblanc said.

"And then, I'm going to do something they won't like at all," Katie said.

"What's that?" Leblanc sounded nervous now.

"I'm going to tell them to call off the race. With two kills so far, in twenty-four hours, it's far too dangerous to continue."

There was a short pause.

"You're right," Leblanc said slowly, shaking his head. "They're not going to like that. Not at all."

CHAPTER FIVE

The race organizer's office was located within the town of Soaring Crow, and Officer Franc accompanied Katie and Leblanc there. Katie noted that it was situated between the town hall and the local community center, which immediately gave her an idea of its importance.

Pushing for this major event to be canceled was not going to be an easy job. In fact, Katie had a strong feeling that the mere suggestion was going to be shot down in flames. She was not going to be popular.

Even so, she resolved to try her hardest. She had no illusions about the consequences if the race and festival went ahead. Unless she and Leblanc got very lucky, very fast, this killer would find it easy to continue with his lethal agenda.

It was simply too dangerous for this event to continue. Katie told herself that firmly, as she got out of the car, shivering in the icy wind that seemed to be a constant fixture – today, at least, and she suspected it was the time of year, also.

The office, in a small, converted house, had laminated notices on the wall outside and a few parking spots, all full. There was a signboard above the main entrance: Race Offices. It was a permanent signboard, smart and wood-framed, not just a temporary one, reinforcing to her that this race was a full-time, year-round project.

People were coming and going through the building's main door. The offices were busy, thronged with competitors and team members. Because of the door opening and closing so often, Katie guessed, they were drafty and chilly.

A stressed-looking woman with dark hair squashed down by a red, woolen hat, was sitting behind the counter on the far side of the lobby. She was typing furiously on a computer keyboard and a printer was whirring.

Voices filled the room, some in different languages. She picked up French, what she guessed was Swedish, and Spanish, as well as a few different colloquial U.S. and Canadian accents. She heard the word 'murder' mentioned a few times as she tuned into the conversations, but it didn't seem as if it was the only topic of discussion. Most of the racers were focused on their goal, she concluded.

While they waited for the people ahead to be helped, Katie saw a notice on the wall, stating that the two main race trophies this year – one for Overall Winner, and one for Best Conditioned Team, were the Togo Trophy and the Balto Trophy. Reading further, she learned these trophies were named after the lead dogs in a team that had transported essential diphtheria medication to the town of Nome, Alaska, in the 1920s, when harsh weather conditions meant that the town could be reached no other way. The teams of heroic sled dogs, tirelessly running hundreds of miles through the freezing wilderness, had saved ten thousand townsfolk who were at risk of annihilation due to the diphtheria epidemic. The story looked interesting, and Katie felt glad to have glanced at it before it was their turn to reach the counter.

Followed by Leblanc and Officer Franc, Katie stepped up and addressed the dark-haired woman.

"We're the investigation team. I'd like to speak to the organizer."

"That's Mr. Pope. He's in the office there. But he's busy!" the woman added, a note of panic in her tone as Katie strode toward the door she'd indicated.

There wasn't time to wait. Risking Mr. Pope's wrath at the interruption, Katie knocked and opened the door, stepping inside.

This office was small and warm. It was dominated by a huge desk, piled with paper and folders. The walls were filled with framed photos of past races. Teams of dogs running through the snow. Winners holding up their trophies in gloved hands, backed by an icy white vista. Groups of dignitaries clustered at the finish line, wrapped in colorful parkas.

Mr. Pope himself was seated behind the desk, talking rapidly on a mobile phone. He was in his forties, Katie judged, with dark, short hair, piercing brown eyes, and a solid build. He had the same tanned, outdoors look she'd noticed in many of the others so far. Most definitely this was no office-bound man, but someone who loved the outdoors and lived the ethos of the area, she decided.

A younger man, in his twenties, who she guessed was his assistant, was hard at work at an adjacent desk, sorting through the files. He had a shock of red hair, and was wearing a hand-knit blue sweater with huskies capering across the chest.

"Mr. Pope?" Katie said politely, as he finished his call and put the phone on the desk.

The dark-haired man looked up, his eyes sharply assessing the incoming trio.

"I'm Katie Winter, FBI. This is Detective Leblanc. Officer Franc brought us here to meet with you, urgently," Katie explained.

"You're here to help with the murders. Of course, of course. Good to meet you."

Standing up, pushing his chair back with some difficulty in the cluttered room, Pope shook their hands. His grip was very firm, his hand warm. "This is Mike, my assistant. I'll give you as much information as you need. It's vital these murders are solved, as we're all extremely concerned, and emotionally, it's taking a toll on our entire community. We've already had sponsors pull out of the race, which is the lifeblood of our town. We're under no illusions how badly this can affect us if it isn't solved soon. What do you want to know?"

Deciding first that she needed to get an overview of the race, Katie asked, "Can you tell me what this festival involves? The timing, duration, number of races?"

"Sure, of course. The race runs over an entire month, starting with the setup, people arriving, acclimatizing, training. Then the races are staggered into different sections and lengths."

"What are those?" Katie asked, eager to learn more.

"There's the sprint race, which is a 20-mile or 30-mile distance - competitors can choose. Then there is the mid-distance race, which this year is being run over a 150-mile track. And finally, there's the long-distance race, which takes competitors all the way over the border into Alaska, and runs over a number of days. It's a true test of endurance, stamina, and fitness. This year, the route is almost 1,000 miles in length and, of course, there are campsites and stop-offs along the way."

That was a long way to ride in the cold, Katie thought, with renewed respect for the teams of dog mushers. No wonder they looked so focused. It had to be their all-consuming passion, she decided.

"After the races, I assume, from looking at this map, that there are other activities planned?" Leblanc asked.

He walked over to a detailed map of the larger site which was pinned to the wall. Katie joined him, feeling glad of the opportunity to orient herself.

The map showed every demarcated area within the grounds where the festival was held. This plot of land adjoined the town itself and connected with it via a short road. The map divided the large festival area into various sections. There were a few different campsites, dog training grounds, an exhibitors' area, the start and finish of the race itself, an outdoor food court, and a medical and veterinary area. Katie noticed other details and structures within this well-located piece of ground that was bordered by thick forest on two sides and, she guessed, was probably at least fifty acres in size.

She could see now what an asset to the town this piece of land was, allowing for easy access to the town itself, while providing a self-contained destination that allowed for hundreds of people to be accommodated.

"After the long-distance race ends, the festival itself kicks off. That's a few days of socializing, events, prize giving ceremonies, parties, awards dinners, as well as some tourist activities. We have VIP guests from all over Canada, Alaska, the rest of the U.S., and other countries in attendance. The sprint races are actually held during the festival as they are easier for the crowds to enjoy, being so short in duration. People drive, ski, and snowshoe out to lookout points to watch the teams go by. We organize shooters, mulled wine, refreshments, and food. It's extremely festive. A lot of people arrive for the finish of the long-distance race, and stay for the festival itself because it really is good fun. An experience. Every year, we strive to make the festival better, and more of a talking point."

Katie raised her eyebrows. "Thanks for the information," she said. It reinforced to her that these distances were vast. And the numbers of races showed her the true scale of the event.

"That's the overview." Pope rubbed his hands together, looking satisfied. "So, tell me, how's the investigation progressing? Do you have a timeline at all, or any leads? We need a very speedy resolution to it. I think at this stage, we're all so inundated that we are trying not to think about what an utter tragedy and catastrophe this is turning out to be."

Katie steeled herself to do what she knew would be best.

"We're actually here for a different reason. We need you to agree to something difficult but necessary."

"What's that?" Pope asked.

"Calling the event off."

Now Pope's eyes widened. "You want us to call off the entire event?"

"It's a question of public safety," Katie said in her most persuasive voice. "We have got a serial killer here, without a doubt. And this event is so big, complex, and widespread, that it's going to be impossible to keep everyone safe."

But already Pope was shaking his head determinedly.

"Absolutely impossible, I'm afraid. Impossible."

"Lives are at risk here," Katie said. "This is not just a question of the sponsors being angry or people being inconvenienced. This is literally a matter of life and death."

Leblanc nodded. "Someone is using this race as a killing ground. We have to put people's safety first."

Pope stared at her and Katie knew from his expression that this man did not consider her to be an ally. He was not on her side, and he was prepared to go head to head with her on this matter.

"I hear you," he said, in a way that told her he might have heard but he was not going to listen. "However, even if we agreed to do such a thing, it's logistically impossible."

"Why's that?" Katie argued.

"Firstly, the competitors in the long-distance race are actually out on the route at the moment. They're arriving back tomorrow afternoon, which is when the festival begins. You can't call off a race that's already in progress. We have literally hundreds of support staff out there, both from the organizers and the different teams."

"But -" Katie started.

Pope raised his hand.

"It's also a case of too many people and too few transportation options. Resources are limited up here. It's a juggling act to get everyone to arrive in time. There are only so many extra flights one can schedule this far north. Only so many bus trips. The presence of all the dogs adds a huge, extra element to what is needed. We literally have attendees arriving and leaving every hour of the day. You cannot just evacuate the area."

"But you could at least shut down where you can. Lock the camping sites down. Get people to stay home. Cancel the shorter races. Just for a day?" Katie implored, but Pope shook his head.

"I'm really sorry, Agent Winter. We have to operate within the realms of what is possible. What you're suggesting is not."

There was an edge of annoyance to his voice, as if he was mad at Katie for having come in with this idea, when he expected her to provide a solution to the case.

At that moment, the door banged open and another man breezed into the small back office. Pope looked relieved to see the man that Katie realized looked like a slightly older version of himself. Pope's next words confirmed this.

"This is Jason. He's my older brother. Jason is the real reason this town has grown. Not me. I'm just the logistics guy. He owns the property."

Katie nodded a greeting at the man who sure looked a lot like Pope, and more good-natured.

"I owned the property. It's the town's property, now." Jason grinned.

"He bought the land up," Pope said. "He had business ideas for it, but in the end he realized what an asset it was to Soaring Crow in terms of its location, and he donated the property to the town."

"Anything that grows the town is good in my book," Jason said. "I'm keen to bring investment here by whatever means it takes. We're fortunate to have some family wealth and investments, and so, what we do is for the good of the town. For our roots, our memories. That land was wasted. It was a mishmash of smaller, neglected properties but in a fabulous location. One by one, we bought them up, and created something really special for Soaring Crow."

Katie found herself smiling, agreeing with what it took to take such a step. Undoubtedly, Jason was a good guy. And that made her feel more positive about Pope. It also made her realize what it would take for him to cancel.

It wasn't just financial interests. It was the love and passion these brothers put into something they thought would grow their hometown. Something which had been done by two people working for good.

But if this continued, it could just as easily destroy it.

"I can't give you more time now, as we're heading to a planning meeting on site, but my phone is always open. Call me at any time. Whatever is possible, I can help with," Pope said firmly. He emphasized the word 'possible' – she guessed, just to make sure that she understood.

Placing a business card in Katie's hand, he strode out with his brother.

Katie sighed.

She'd received nothing less than a firm no, and now realized that Pope considered the police to be causing interference and obstructions, rather than working in the interests of saving lives. She did, however, see his point that the logistics made this difficult.

"Even some shutdown would help," Leblanc grumbled, clearly unsatisfied with this result, as they filed out of the small office.

"If he won't agree, we can't force it," Katie said. "But it's going to make our job more difficult, that's for sure. Seeing this has turned into a dead end, let's head straight to Thomas's family, now, and see if there are any leads from that side. Perhaps he picked up that something was wrong, or noticed someone behaving strangely, and told his father or his sister before he died."

CHAPTER SIX

Katie couldn't help feeling frustrated as she climbed into the SUV with Leblanc. That meeting with the race organizer had been unproductive. The suggestion of shutting any part of the race down had been met with firm resistance.

Pope was clearly appalled by the very idea, which she did acknowledge was frighteningly complex.

She wondered if he would be forced to rethink if the worst happened, and the killer struck again. If this happened, which she prayed it wouldn't – but if it did, she was going to be straight back in that office, asking him again.

For now, though, they needed to see if there was any way to find out who the killer was.

"Thomas's sister lives next door to him," Leblanc saw, reading through the case file. "And his father lives a couple of streets away. It's just ten minutes from where we are now."

"We can probably drop you off on the way," Katie said to Officer Franc. With the race continuing, she knew that he would have his work cut out for him keeping things safe. Now that they had an idea of the town's layout and the race logistics, he needed to get back to his job.

"That'll be great," Franc said, sounding relieved, and Katie guessed he also wasn't looking forward to what the next few days might bring.

She detoured to the police department - which was on the other end of Soaring Crow's main road - and after dropping Franc there, she headed to the address of Thomas's sister.

Cayleigh Briggs lived on one of Soaring Crow's side streets, a scenic road that was bordered by snowy forests. When Katie pulled up outside the single-story home, she saw a couple of cars parked outside.

"I hope this means that some of Thomas's friends, and maybe his father, are here, too," she said to Leblanc as they climbed out and trudged along the freshly dug pathway, to the front door.

"Yes. The more different versions we can get in the shortest time, the better," he agreed.

Katie felt grateful beyond words to be working with Leblanc. It was amazing, now, how easily they worked together and how in tune they were.

Yet again, she suppressed a pang of regret that she had not pursued their romance. She was filled with self-doubt when she thought about it. Had she given up too soon? Was this the result of a flaw in herself that she should have tried to fix? What was he thinking? Had he accepted this, or did he feel resentment and regret?

Shaking her head slightly to try and dislodge these uncomfortable thoughts, Katie knocked on the home's gray wooden door.

Footsteps sounded, and a moment later, it opened.

In the doorway stood a woman who looked to be in her early forties. She was plump and round-faced, with pale, flawless, and un-weathered skin that told Katie that the outdoors wasn't really her thing. However, her cheeks were flushed and her eyes reddened, evidence that she'd taken this death hard.

"Agent Winter and Detective Leblanc," Katie introduced them, feeling a pang of sympathy for this obviously distressed woman. "Are you Thomas's sister?"

"I'm Cayleigh Briggs, yes," she said. "Please come in. It's a little crowded. My dad's here, and a couple of my friends. I - I'm so traumatized by this. I hope you can find answers."

Turning, she stumbled through the tiny hallway, and into a small living room where two people sat - one an older man with gray hair, who must be Thomas's father. Three more people were milling round, organizing coffee, putting out platters of snacks. There was a slightly desperate feeling, Katie sensed, of comfort being offered by whatever means possible. Again, she felt painful regret at the circumstances that had claimed this man's life. They really needed to move fast on this, because with the organizer's refusal to cancel the race, there was even more of a sense of urgency surrounding the case. They had to catch this killer before he struck again.

"The police are here," Cayleigh blurted out, collapsing down on the sofa beside her father.

Everyone turned to look at Katie and Leblanc, and Katie saw a variety of expressions. One or two of the crowd looked grateful. The others looked suspicious.

Katie was used to this. Even when murders had occurred, law enforcement in these areas was not always welcome. She knew people's preconceptions were deeply ingrained, and often linked to a distrust of the police.

"We need to ask a few questions to help us find this killer," Katie said calmly, deciding to put into place a logical triage system. "I think we need to speak to everyone who spoke to Thomas in the last few days. If you had any conversation with him, please stay in this room. If you haven't spoken to Thomas directly, recently, then I'm going to ask you to step out for a moment."

There was a silence.

Then three of the guests shuffled out, leaving behind Cayleigh, her father, and a middle-aged woman with a square face and short, brown-gray hair.

"I'm Helen, Thomas's neighbor on the other side," the woman introduced herself. "He and I did speak yesterday, but briefly."

They all sat down, meaning that every chair in the room was now occupied.

"Did he tell you where he was going?" Katie asked Helen. "We need to know how and where this could have happened."

"His car was still in the garage. But he didn't use it for trips within town. He liked to walk. He'd walk to the shops, and walk out to the bars and restaurants, which are not too far away," Helen explained.

"There was no sign of a break in or anything at home. He just wasn't there in the morning, and we hadn't even started thinking something was wrong, when we got the call from the police," Cayleigh said.

"Thomas was a local businessman, am I correct?" Katie asked, wanting to find out more about his role in the community.

Cayleigh nodded. "He was the town's notary. Everyone used him. He was the go-to man. He was well-known and well-liked."

"Any conflicts, personal or business?" Leblanc asked.

Cayleigh shook her head firmly. "Absolutely not. He really was, like, a pillar of the community. One of those people who always acts with integrity. Just a really nice person." She sniffed again, and Helen reached forward and passed her a box of Kleenex.

"Did Thomas mention anything unusual, anything disturbing, happening in the past few days?" Katie said.

She looked at the trio closely but saw no immediate signs that anyone had anything on their mind.

"How do you mean?" Thomas's father said carefully.

"Perhaps he noticed someone loitering around, perhaps his car or home was broken into, perhaps he thought he was being followed?"

She tried to keep the questions open, in order that they might spark a thought or memory in the three people opposite her.

Helen sighed. "I guess you're asking if he might have sensed someone was preparing to attack him? Maybe staking him out?"

"Exactly," Katie said.

But Helen shook her head. "I wish I could tell you something helpful, but when I spoke to him over the fence yesterday morning, he didn't mention a thing."

His father nodded. "We live in a peaceful place. I must say, I spoke to him on the phone a couple of times in the past few days, and he said that work was very busy, there was a lot of business being done. It was keeping his time occupied, as was the volunteering to help at the race. But nothing like what you've mentioned."

"If there had been anything, I'm not sure he would have told us," Cayleigh said. "He was not one of those people who panics over things. He would probably just have noticed it, and waited to see if anything further happened. He was quite protective over his family. Not one of those who overshares."

"Did he mention if he was meeting anyone, or seeing anyone, last night?"

Three headshakes indicated that she wasn't going to get an answer to this important question.

Katie felt disappointed. If this was Thomas's character, it was likely that he might have kept something suspicious to himself. They were not going to get lucky here, that was for sure.

"Tell me more about the volunteering," she tried. "How was he helping with the race?"

"He was on the committee that helped to organize accommodations for the racers in town. There's often a lot of last-minute changes and places needed. So there's a committee that deals with it and sources extra places to stay. But I don't see how that could make anyone want to kill him."

"It might be important, so thank you for mentioning it," Katie said, even though she couldn't see how this could have caused trouble in any way.

They would have to dig further and think harder for the answers, but none were to be found here, in this small and humble home, where sadness still hung heavy in the air.

"Thank you so much for your time," Katie said. "Please call me if you think of anything, or remember anything that might help."

She stood up and handed them her business card, but as she did so, her phone started ringing. It was the hospital on the line, and that meant there was news on Josie.

Why were they calling? Had something gone wrong? Or was this to say that increasing the doses of the most recent treatment had worked at last?

Glancing apologetically at Leblanc, she rushed out, anxiety flaring, ready to take the call.

CHAPTER SEVEN

"Hello? Doctor Andrews?" Katie recognized his extension number. The doctor was calling personally. She was filled with worry about what he would say.

"Agent Winter. Do you have a moment?" The doctor's tone sounded neutral. Katie had no idea if it was going to be good or bad news. She gripped the phone hard, staring out at the narrow, snow-flanked road.

"I do," she said.

"Unfortunately," the doctor began, and Katie's heart dropped like a stone. This one word signaled that it was bad news. She fought for calmness, to accept the bombshell, to listen carefully and with a clear mind in case decisions were necessary.

"Unfortunately, your sister has not responded well to higher doses of the new drug that we were using. We're taking a big step back and re-looking at this treatment plan completely, because she actually experienced what we could describe as a psychotic episode."

"A psychotic episode?" Katie said, her voice incredulous. She hadn't thought this nightmare could deepen, but reality was proving to her that there were literally no limits to how bad things could get. She thought of the terror and confusion which must have gripped her sister and her heart felt as if it was wrenching in her chest.

"Yes. She was hallucinating, without a doubt. It almost seemed she was reliving an incident in her past, probably something that occurred during her ordeal of being held captive."

"Oh, no," Katie whispered.

"She went into a hysterical fit. Then she became very aggressive and literally tried to attack her own face, to rip at her own skin and eyes. Thankfully, one of the nurses was able to grab her just in time, before anything happened. We have her in padded restraints now. But she is a danger to herself, as well as others. She's receiving close observation again. We're monitoring her around the clock. We're going to keep her sedated for the rest of the day. It is vital she gets rest, but at some stage she will have to wake up and then we'll be back to square

34

one, or even square minus one, depending on what happens when we assess her again."

"This is such a setback," Katie said, feeling as if she had been punched hard in the stomach. "That's not good, Doc."

"No, it isn't," Doctor Andrews agreed. "It's not good at all. At the moment, there are no physical impairments. She's in good health, although she risks jeopardizing her health when this happens. But her mind is not working properly."

"So what are you saying?" Katie asked, feeling helpless. "What do we do?"

"To be honest, we don't know," the doctor said, his tone grave. "This medication was our last resort. I'm going to put her back on the old drug, just to keep her stable, but it's the one that she was regressing on. So it looks as if the ECT that we discussed earlier today might end up being necessary sooner rather than later. Just for her own safety, and also the safety of the staff who are caring for her."

"I see," Katie said, feeling traumatized and helpless. If this was the only thing that might work, then there was no other solution, but it worried her deeply that treatments that were supposed to work had already sent Josie off on the opposite end of the scale. If this did the same, they would have checkmated themselves, especially with the associated risks of brain damage and memory loss.

"How long do we have to decide?" she asked.

"A couple of days, at most. With any luck, this original treatment can at least slow down her regression again. But we're going to have to make a call on this very soon. The only other alternative is to get her committed to a psychiatric care unit as a long-term patient. When her health improves, that's something we can consider, but I don't think it's the best option for now, it's only a solution if all else really does fail."

Katie pressed her lips together. She didn't think that would be the right thing. Doing that would mean admitting that they had all given up on the idea of her recovery and were now just looking to manage her problems as best they could. She didn't think that environment would be conducive to healing in any way.

"Thanks for the update and for explaining the timeframe," she said, forcing herself to sound brisk and matter of fact, even though inside she felt like screaming.

"Let me know tomorrow what your decision is. Sorry for the bad news. The team is taking it very personally. Everyone who works with her is invested in her recovery. This has been a hard thing to deal with."

The doctor disconnected.

Katie looked around to see Leblanc staring at her, looking worried. He must have heard the last part of her conversation.

"I'm so sorry," he muttered.

"I can't take this." Katie took a shaky breath. Tears were threatening, but she knew if she started crying now, there'd be no way she'd stop.

Her sister was on a path to disaster, misery, being permanently institutionalized.

She hadn't expected this. She'd hoped they were close to a breakthrough, that somehow, her own force of will and desire for Josie to get better, could blast healing vibes through the damage and trauma.

Now, she had to admit that all her good intentions, all the determination and love in the world, was useless. Her twin sister was too seriously affected.

"Let's take a walk," she said, not wanting to get back in the car now, but needing to clear her mind and refocus. "I need some air right now. There's a path going down there into the woods. We can speak about the case while we go."

"Good idea," Leblanc said. Like her, she knew, he was also someone who preferred action and movement to being huddled over an office desk. As she strode down the path, with the icy breeze caressing her face, Katie tried her best to get her thoughts back into order.

"From what we've seen, it doesn't look like Thomas saw anything," Katie summarized, thinking back on what they'd recently been told.

"No. And no trouble going on in his life."

They had reached the trees now. The path wound in between the tall, snowy pines, and she picked up on the immediate stillness that their cover brought. They walked in silence for a while. Katie's mind was full of questions, but she couldn't think of a scenario that made sense.

"He was on the committee organizing accommodations for the dog sled festival," Katie said thoughtfully. "Do you think that was a reason?"

"Especially since both these victims were involved with this race, and the festival, in various ways," Leblanc said. "Perhaps it is significant."

"Well, for now, it's the only common factor."

"And unfortunately, it's a very common factor. The majority of the town is involved in this event, in one way or another. It could just be the law of averages." Hands buried in his pockets, Leblanc strode beside her, his face somber.

"Or maybe it's more intentional than that." Katie mused, taking the idea further, working with it, seeing if it might lead anywhere. "Because what if this killer's purpose is to sabotage the race? And he's achieving his goal by the murders?"

"By killing people who are associated with it?"

"Yes. What if that's his reason?"

"It's a possibility," Leblanc said, glancing around. There was a crossroads ahead, and another path leading out of the woods. They took it, heading on a winding route back to the road.

"We're saying 'he' for now," Katie said. "But it could also be a very strong woman? Moving the bodies in the snow would be hard work, but we can't rule it out."

She recalled what the coroner had said. The victims were knocked out, moved, and then their throats were slashed to bleed out in the snow. So man or woman, the perpetrator would be fit and strong.

"We can't rule much out at this point," Leblanc agreed in a resigned tone.

"If that is his purpose, or her purpose, there would be a motive behind it," Katie said. "Whoever is doing this would need to have a serious issue with the race. They would have had to reach the stage in their own mind where they believe the only solution is to commit a series of murders to get it shut down."

They were both walking faster now, warming up and more energized.

"That would mean the killer is someone who knows the race, who is familiar with it, and with the dog sledding world," Leblanc said.

"Maybe a local, or maybe someone who has traveled here for this reason, to kill."

"You know who always seems to know about things like this? Issues that arise?" Leblanc said.

Katie gave the answer before he'd even spoken it.

"The local press," she said.

"Exactly," Leblanc said.

She nodded, now feeling as if they had a solid new direction to explore.

"The local press will know if there's any resistance to the race. Anyone who's tried to shut it down, complained, demonstrated, or tried to sabotage it in the past. I think our next stop should be their offices. Everyone in town wants this race - except for a few who have their own reasons for hating it. Isn't it always that way?"

"We need to find out who those few are," Leblanc agreed, as they strode purposefully back to the car.

CHAPTER EIGHT

The weather was getting colder, a bitter northerly breeze was surging. Out here, in the empty park, lined with a row of dark, rustling pines, the wind felt like icy knives. But in his heart, the man in the coat was not cold. Instead, he felt as if he was burning with the need to complete his mission.

He waited, in the car near the corner of the street, looking out at the suburban landscape. It was like any other – trees, roads, homes, and parks – although colder than most. Snow covered every surface, making it seem both beautiful and strangely bleak.

Thinking of that beauty, that bleakness, that space, gave the man in the coat a sudden, painful pang of loss.

But then, with a shake of his head, he set the feeling aside. The time for feelings was over. Now, action had started and the payback he'd longed for was rolling out.

He got out of his car, locked it behind him, and then jogged across the road to the park.

He walked through the row of pines, and turned the corner, heading deeper into the park. The ground was uneven in this small forest, a carpet of frozen leaves and pine needles that bent and cracked under his boots. He could smell the pines, mingled with the dampness of the earth and the snow. It was an enjoyable walk through this frigid but scenic area, although not just a random one, because he had a very important purpose.

He opened up his coat, letting the cold slap against his plaid shirt. Like the coat, it was cheap, plain, the fabric in muted grays and browns. Invisible and forgettable. He didn't wear bright colors. Not anymore.

And definitely not now, because now it was important that he wasn't noticed. Where he was heading and where he was going, he needed to remain unseen.

Luckily, the man knew exactly where he was heading. He had a target in mind.

Not just any target, but a very carefully researched target. There was an important, logical reason why this target was being chosen next, and the man in the coat felt triumphant and intent as he headed along the route.

He was on his way to the home of the local lawyer, Ivan Menzies.

The man in the coat knew everything about Ivan Menzies. Where he lived. What he did.

This kill would necessitate a deviation from his previous hunting ground because Ivan Menzies was not involved in the Sled Dog Festival this year, like his previous two victims were. He was one of the few, it seemed, not caught up in the whirl of excitement surrounding this event.

The man in the coat walked on, down the small path, until he came to the back of the house he knew Ivan Menzies occupied. He stood there, taking a few minutes to watch the home, looking for any signs of movement, any evidence that the man was inside.

Ivan was a hard man, one of those men who looked at you, and you saw dollar signs in his eyes. He was all about closing the deal, billing the hours. There was not a shred of humanity in this man, and never had been, the man in the coat knew. Although all his targets had to die, there would be a particular pleasure in making this kill. It was, after all, such a deserving target.

The man in the coat smiled.

This would be the next step in his master plan, the next act in his revenge saga.

He had the entire sequence of events worked out in his mind, including the moving and the placement of the body before he made the final kill, which was, of course, vital. Nobody knew or guessed why, which he found rather amusing. They never would. Only he knew the deep significance behind each murder.

They would be running around in circles, panicking, blaming the wrong people. Perhaps the festival would get called off, although he doubted that. He'd seen already what a juggernaut was created by the driving force of financial interest and unfettered greed. It was a runaway truck with no brakes.

Oh, but it would crash and burn, he would make sure of that.

Here was Menzies's house. A fancy house, one of the best in the area. Most definitely the highest caliber of home that money could buy. Money, money, money, the man thought sourly, as he looked at the

40

home, with its white painted walls and its ostentatiously pillared porch, even though the number of days when you could actually sit out on a porch in this cold area were probably in the tens, every year. In the tens. The low tens. Laughable, really, what people did in order to flaunt their wealth and impress.

He didn't stride up onto the porch although the idea was compelling, simply to march up as if he owned it. But caution was key. And he was aware of the need to take basic precautions, such as not being noticed, and not leaving footprints.

Luckily, the path was swept and the snow had been piled roughly around the porch. It had then frozen solid into ice. It was a slippery surface, but he knew from long experience in this area that it would be way too hard to hold the footprint of the perfectly average boots he wore - a size too large, with two pairs of thick socks, just in case. He imagined a policeman, with an expression of concentration on his dull, aggressive face, measuring the prints if he did find them. The bigger shoe size, while perfectly fine to walk in, would undoubtedly lead him the wrong way, and that was just one precaution among many he was taking.

Because he intended to be careful every step of the way. His mission must go seamlessly and he did not intend to make a mistake or leave any evidence behind.

He listened carefully, pressing himself close to the home's back door. There was always the chance Menzies would be home and then he would have to recalibrate his plans. But he should not be. The man in the coat knew that. It was a matter of watching and waiting. He had been waiting for a while now to get the correct timing.

The perfect time.

It was a matter of patience, and patience was an asset the man in the coat was well acquainted with.

Like pain and suffering.

Those, he also knew too well. They were familiar companions, and now the time had come to finally exorcise these demons.

He waited out the time, watching the house for even the smallest sign of life.

This kill needed to fit in with his planned timeframe, and he intended to take this man when he came home, which should be at around eight p.m. After dark. And after a visit to the bar where he liked to go after work, to drink three or four beers before driving home. He shouldn't drive after drinking that much, but somehow for people like him, there were never consequences.

Until now.

Menzies would be alone when he got back. That was because he'd cheated on his wife last year and she now lived two streets down. The whole town knew about that. Word traveled fast. But he hadn't become a pariah, oh no. People with money and influence never did. The town had conveniently forgotten about his misdoings, although the man in the coat had not.

That wasn't why he was going to be sacrificed, though. There was a different reason for that.

And he couldn't wait to explain it to him, even though Menzies would be unconscious at the time before he delivered the killing slice that would spill his blood onto the ground. The explanation would feel cathartic, and that was what mattered.

Smiling, he drew a thin blade from his pocket, and then carefully, slowly, he inserted the tip inside the lock, observing the resistance of the tumbler. He pushed, feeling the mechanism inside the keyhole give slightly, the tumbler releasing.

And then, as silent as a shadow, the man in the coat stepped inside the home, to wait.

CHAPTER NINE

The Soaring Crow Community Media Center was a long name for a very small business, Katie thought, climbing the narrow, rickety staircase to the upstairs room in the town's community center.

This was where the media operated, and from what Leblanc had been able to ascertain on his phone while Katie drove, the media included a bi-monthly newspaper, a website, and a social media page for community news and sponsored updates.

Climbing the last of the wobbly wooden stairs, Katie came face to face with the team - consisting of a serious looking woman in her thirties, with short, bleached hair, wearing a fluffy turquoise coat, and an older woman with gray, braided hair, and dark eyes.

"Good afternoon," Katie greeted the duo, moving aside so that Leblanc could step off the creaky wooden treads and onto the wooden floorboards. The ceiling rafters were so low that her tall investigation partner had to bend his head down, but the tiny office looked full of activity. There were three open laptops, a whiteboard on the wall with notes and jottings, several open files on the desk, and numerous posters on the walls, which all seemed to be of events or initiatives that the Soaring Crow media had been involved in.

A tiny window gave a surprisingly beautiful view of the snow-covered houses, with fields and mountains beyond.

"Good afternoon," the woman with bleached hair greeted them. "Are you in the right place? You're looking for the news offices?"

Clearly she'd pegged them as police, despite the fact neither were in uniform. Katie showed her badge all the same, to complete the formalities.

"That's correct. We're investigating the murders."

The woman with braided hair looked up, her eyes sharp, as if hoping to get the inside scoop on the latest developments.

"I'm Winona North, the media owner, and this is Nanouk, our journalist and assistant," the bleached haired woman said. "I must say, this has happened at a really bad time, with the festival taking place."

She stared at them inquiringly.

"We're investigating the possibility that someone might want to sabotage the festival or the race," Katie said.

"You'd better sit down," Winona said.

She exchanged a glance with Nanouk. Katie took the offered seat, a small office chair with no armrests, and Leblanc sat down on a similar one.

"This is a very serious line of thought, and a difficult question to answer," Winona said. "Basically, you're wondering if someone might have actually done this for the sole purpose of sabotaging the race and festival?" She sounded puzzled, as if battling to understand why anyone would do such a thing.

"The Sled Dog Festival benefits the entire town," Nanouk said gently.

Katie nodded. "Yes, it does. We're merely exploring every possibility. Whoever committed this crime is going to the extreme, and they certainly won't be a normal member of society, even if they might act like one. But behind every serial murder there is a motive, even if it makes sense to the killer only."

Now, the two women were looking less confused, and more cooperative. Winona tipped her head in understanding.

"If we can uncover a motive, then we might be able to work our way back to the killer. And as the local media, you're in the loop," Katie said. "I am sure you're the first port of call when anyone wants to complain, question something, or report something irregular going on. Most probably, you get contacted before the police do."

Winona gave a short laugh, and then quickly stopped herself, as if feeling embarrassed that she'd shown such emotion at such a serious time. "Sorry," she said. "But that's true. Half the calls we get, we refer them straight to the police. There's often nothing we can do story-wise, until a formal complaint or charge has been made."

"We rarely write stories based on rumors," Nanouk said quietly, with a flash of defiance in her eyes. "We don't print any stories without facts. We don't make things up. We wouldn't get anyone to read us or respect us if we did."

"But do you take their details when people call, even if you can't take the story forward? Or maybe, in a small town, you must know who's complaining and why?" Leblanc queried, raising his eyebrows.

"Yes. Most of the time, we do," Winona said slowly.

"Do you know anyone who might hold a grudge against the festival, or the people who were involved in the organizing of the event?" Katie asked. "Anyone who, for whatever reason, has caused trouble there?"

"A personal grudge?"

Katie shrugged. "Personal, ethical, who knows? But people are never unanimous. There must be a few who had issues with the festival, even if the reasons didn't make total sense."

Winona sighed. Katie guessed she might have someone in mind as she turned to her laptop and began scrolling through something Katie couldn't see, narrowing her eyes as she went. Katie guessed she was looking up records or old stories to confirm this theory.

"You know, this can put us in a difficult situation," Winona said reluctantly, turning back to Katie. "We keep our sources confidential. Being a small town, you can't really afford to make enemies if you're a business. And that includes us. We don't hesitate to publish controversial issues, but we do try to keep confidentiality when people complain."

Katie sensed resistance. She got the strong feeling Winona was backing away, that she didn't want to get involved if the lines were drawn and it was town versus police.

She tried again, hoping she could use a different argument to persuade this clearly intelligent woman.

"People never complain to just one person. And this being a small town, by the time the complaint reaches you, it's probably gone past several friends, neighbors, colleagues, family. There are no big secrets here, correct?"

She waited, hoping that her words would make sense to the two women.

"Of course, that's true," Nanouk agreed thoughtfully. "A lot of what we hear and what we're told is based in gossip." She looked at Katie and Leblanc, shrugging.

"Murder has the potential to destroy this town and this festival if it happens again, and the problem with a serial killer is that they take multiple victims," Katie said. "This hasn't stopped. It's only just started."

Winona sighed. "If possible, please don't say that this came from the media. If they ask, I would rather that you say you heard it via the grapevine or that someone else told you."

45

Katie felt a flare of triumph because this showed that Winona was going to agree. She'd set her reservations aside, and was going to cooperate.

"We did have one serious complaint recently and they wanted us to do a story, but we ended up with insufficient proof. I won't tell you who complained, but I can tell you who the complaint was about. Because that might provide a direction you could take."

Katie sat up straighter. Finally, they were getting somewhere.

"Last year, we received a tip-off that someone tried to sabotage the race by damaging some of the sleds. Luckily the damage was detected and they were fixed before the race began. There wasn't enough evidence to link back to this person. But this year, she's here again. We had two people call in yesterday and tell us."

"And who is she? Why the sabotage?"

"She's a woman who lives in a neighboring town. Her name's Julia Marr. And she's an animal rights activist. She thinks dog racing is cruel and abusive to the dogs. She wants the race shut down. She's said so, outspokenly, to us and to others. And so, in turn, people have complained about her."

"Julia Marr?" Katie asked. "Which town does she live in?"

"Cobalt, about two hundred miles south of here. I don't know more than that."

"We don't need more. And I really appreciate the lead. We'll keep your name confidential," Katie promised.

She stood up, feeling enthused. An animal rights activist with a history of sabotage?

They might have found their killer already.

CHAPTER TEN

Katie left the local media offices, clambering carefully down the wobbly stairs, but feeling a lot more positive than she had when they arrived. Already, she was assessing the information on their strong suspect, Julia Marr.

She'd tried to sabotage the race in the past although there was no official police record proving her guilt. However, from her actions, she had a strong motive to want to stop it. In her own mind, this woman believed racing was cruel.

If Julia Marr was a psychopath who held these beliefs, her agenda could easily have escalated to murder.

"Cobalt is a long drive from here," Leblanc observed, as they walked out of the community hall. From his tone of voice, Katie could already tell he was thinking what she was.

"It will probably be a wasted drive," she said.

"Exactly. If Julia is the one committing these murders, she's not there. She's here. But even so, we need to contact the local RCMP offices in Cobalt. They can take a drive past her house and confirm that. We could also check with the organizers here. She might have booked accommodations under her own name, although of course there are ways of getting around that if she wanted to stay here without people knowing."

Katie wanted to pursue both lines of research in case one didn't pan out.

"I'll call the RCMP now," Leblanc said.

"I'll do some research and see what visuals we can get on her," Katie said. If she was a known animal rights activist, photos might well be out in the public domain. At the very least, she could call up her ID details from the official records.

As soon as they got into the car, Katie turned it on and cranked up the heater. Even with it going full blast, it took a few minutes for the car to reach the temperature where she could take her gloves off without her fingers turning numb. It really was freezing this far north and Katie could see why they'd timed the festival to occur right at the end of the cold season.

The excitement and activity must be a huge motivator, lifting spirits and bringing hope after the seemingly endless winter.

Once she'd defrosted, she went looking for the visuals, immersed in her task, barely aware of Leblanc making his cellphone call in the passenger seat.

She had to wade through a lot of information on the first search engine she tried, but eventually she found a picture of Julia Marr.

The photo was taken in front of the Soaring Crow community hall. Julia, wearing a heavy parka, a warm knit hood, and sturdy boots, was holding up a handwritten protest sign in her gloved hands.

"Save the Sled Dogs," it read.

Katie zoomed in to try and make out Julia's features under all those coverings. One thing she could tell immediately, from the scale of the photo, was that she looked to be tall. She was not a petite woman. Katie assessed that Julia would have had the strength to commit the murders.

But did she have the resolve? Could they link her to the crimes?

She had a pretty face, with wavy brown hair peeking out from her knit hat, and a strong, determined looking jaw.

It wasn't a lot to go on - but Katie acknowledged that in a race environment where everyone was wrapped up in all the coverings they had, it was all they were going to get.

This is why I wanted to get this damned event called off, she thought to herself, feeling frustrated all over again that her request had been refused.

Leblanc got off the phone.

"The local RCMP has just taken a drive past her house. She lives a couple of blocks from their department. Sounds like everything is a couple of blocks from everything else in that small town."

"Is she there?"

"No sign of her, they said."

Katie shook her head. "She's here. I know it. She's here. This is her."

She showed Leblanc the photo.

"She's not exactly keeping a low profile." He frowned down at the screen.

"She might be now."

He sighed. "True. Now that we know she's not back home, I can check the bookings and see if we can find out where she's staying."

"That can be one alternative. To go and check with them, and track her down where she's staying."

"And the other?" Leblanc asked.

"The other would simply be to go out and look for her," Katie said. "Because I doubt she'll be inside right now. She'll be out, seeking new targets, doing her research, staking out victims."

"The day's nearly over. It's late afternoon now and there's not much daylight left," Leblanc observed.

"I agree. We don't have time to spare, so I think we need to work separately from each other, for now."

"I'll start with the research," Leblanc offered.

"And I'll start by searching in the crowds," Katie said. "I guess the campsite and training area, where there are kiosks and activities set up, will be the best place to start. That's where most of the crowds are. And both the bodies, so far, have been dumped within this festival area."

She took another look at the photo, taking in the details. The color of the hair, the shape of the face. Also, the clothing. Julia Marr's outfit looked new in the photo, and she might be wearing the same parka or the same hat this time around, so Katie committed those to memory too, and sent the photo to Leblanc.

Then they drove the short distance out of town to the main race grounds, and parked in the visitor's parking, joining about a hundred other vehicles already there.

Katie climbed out, ready for the hunt.

She set off at a fast walk to her right, heading for the camp and training areas. She walked past the registration kiosks, the food tents, and the public toilets. The campsite and race area seemed to be on a very well located piece of land, she saw. It was large, flat, scenic, and with a thick bank of pine forest to the north, making it more sheltered from the wind than other areas.

Already there was a vibe, with music playing from somewhere, people lining up for coffee, and the pop-up bar in a temporary wooden structure doing a good trade. There were people walking dogs everywhere. There were tents, stalls, and kiosks set up offering all kinds of equipment, clothing, training accessories, harness items, and more.

Katie slowed her pace, looking around, scanning the clusters of people. She was looking for something that stood out, something that caught her eye. Julia Marr wasn't here to socialize or enjoy herself. Her body language would be different from the others, and Katie knew that if she was perceptive enough, that could be her first clue.

Ahead, she heard the ringing of bells, and saw to her surprise that dog sled rides were being offered to the public, over a two-mile track.

There was a long line for this activity, with cheerful people talking and laughing as they waited.

Remembering the issues that Julia had with the dogs being raced, Katie wondered if this might be a good place to look for her. Perhaps she was around here, planning her next kill, picking out a victim while keeping a watchful eye on the well-being of the dogs to fuel her murderous intentions.

Katie headed over, weaving her way through the throngs, waiting to pick up the subtle signs that might signal to her that a killer was lurking.

She heard the jingle of bells, and breathed in the rich aroma of burgers being cooked on a gas fire at the food kiosk. There were other dishes, too, for those who didn't want to opt for such conventional fare. Notices on wooden stakes stuck into hay bales outside the stalls advertised Alaskan king crab legs, smoked salmon chowder, hot dogs with reindeer sausage, berry crisp. As she walked down the line of stalls, the scents were mouthwatering.

A burst of laughter came from the bar area. Someone jostled her shoulder and apologized, turning back to converse with his friend again. She took a look at the sleds themselves, realizing that apart from those cheerful bells, they were very basic. She guessed they had to be lightweight so that the dogs could pull them for so many miles. They seemed to consist of a platform in front, and then a standing area at the back, where the driver stood, holding onto the highest part of the sled's frame, and directed the dogs.

And then, as she took in the design and logistics of the sleds, Katie saw something that alerted her.

A woman, with her back to Katie, about thirty yards away, standing apart from the others, was watching the dog racing with a strange intensity.

There was something about her body language that Katie noticed, a stillness to her, a focus.

She was tall, broad shouldered, and wearing what looked to be the same parka, a pale blue garment. She turned her head slightly and Katie paused, straining her eyes against the glare of sun on snow, looking to see if she could pick up any features.

She caught a glimpse of dark, wavy hair.

Katie's pulse accelerated. This looked identical to the picture she'd seen. She could be staring directly at the suspect they needed.

Quickly, Katie moved forward, but at that moment, the woman turned away, moving fast, melting into the crowds that were thronging to and from the campsite, so that in a moment, Katie lost sight of her.

She couldn't afford to lose this woman now.

Katie broke into a run, pounding across the snow, searching for any glimpse of that pale blue garment, of the quick way that the woman had stepped over the snow in her fur boots.

There she was!

She was heading down, past the tents, along a path that seemed to lead away from the camping ground.

"Hey! Wait a moment, please," Katie called, jogging along the path after her. "Wait up, I'd like to speak to you."

The woman glanced around.

She saw Katie.

"Police," Katie called.

But the woman didn't stop. Instead, she broke into a full run, her long legs scissoring, sprinting past the campsite, and heading for a trail leading to the forest. In a moment, she was going to disappear into the dark cover of the woods.

Swearing, Katie set off in pursuit.

CHAPTER ELEVEN

Leblanc strode into the organizer's offices, which were as busy as when they'd been in there recently. Weaving the way through the crowds, he headed purposefully to the front desk. He was as sure as Katie was that Julia Marr was a likely suspect, and certain that she was lurking around the campsite or the race area, looking for an opportunity to strike another blow against this perceived cruelty.

If she was resorting to murder, then every second counted in locating her.

Feeling resolute, Leblanc stood at the desk and waited for the busy assistant to turn to him.

"I'm looking to see if there is accommodation booked in a certain name," he said.

He showed his badge, just as a reminder this was police business.

"What name is that?" the attendant asked, looking dubious, as if she suspected this was going to cause some kind of trouble.

"Julia Marr," he said.

"Julia Marr." Her eyes narrowed and Leblanc saw the name was familiar to her. Most likely, the race organizers had heard of the links to the sabotage last year, not to mention the demonstrations outside their offices. So he had a feeling that giving the details wouldn't be a problem for her, and sure enough, muttering the name under her breath she turned to the second of the two computer screens.

"She's booked into Pine Tree House," the attendant said.

"Where's that located?" That needed to be his first stop, Leblanc decided.

"That's a chalet in the residential section on the west side. They're all named after trees there. But I'm afraid you can't just go in there. It's one of our ladies' chalets, where the bedrooms are rented out by women attending the festival. So there are strict rules that no non-residents can have access." She sounded disappointed, as if she would have liked Leblanc to storm in there and drag this trouble-causer out by the collar of her parka.

"Can you show me on the map where it is?" Leblanc asked. He might not need to go in, but it would be a good starting point from which to track her.

"Sure. I can show you." She pointed on the map.

"Thanks," Leblanc said, walking quickly out of the hubbub of the organizer's office, and heading over the icy road in the direction of the camping grounds and race venue.

As he strode along, keeping a picture in his mind of where the chalet was, he couldn't help his thoughts straying to Katie.

He had to admit, his thoughts had a tendency to do that. Every time he thought about Katie, he had to remind himself that they were not a couple, they were no longer an item. She'd needed her space and had called off their budding romance. Leblanc respected her wishes but he deeply regretted the decision. He couldn't help thinking of her still with respect, affection - and with desire.

And yet, he knew that she had more than enough on her plate and that her sister's ordeal must be emotionally shattering for her. Leblanc was starting to harbor private fears that Josie might never come right. If she didn't, he knew that Katie would suffer a whole new level of stress and self-blame, and he worried how it would affect her both personally and as a team member.

Leblanc sighed, wishing that life didn't have to be so damned complicated. Why did the road to happiness sometimes seem as if it was paved with rocks, he wondered. Would they ever be able to get together romantically again? He couldn't help hoping this might happen.

For now, there was no point in agonizing over the situation anymore. Not when he was now approaching the chalet itself, set in a quiet and secluded part of the large, attractive venue grounds.

It was a cold and still afternoon, the trees and shrubbery were gilded with last night's snow, and the area seemed quiet and peaceful. There were a couple of lights on inside the chalet and he wondered if Julia was in there.

But respect for rules was important, and Leblanc did not want to transgress those rules.

Instead, he surveyed the wider area and took a look at where Julia could potentially have gone from this starting point. Was there a reason why she'd booked a room in this chalet? Was there a vantage point that she wanted to access or stake out? It was within a few hundred yards of where both the murders had occurred.

Leblanc paced around the split pole fence that bordered the chalet, scanning the view. If she was in fact responsible for the deaths, then Leblanc had to figure out where she might have gone from here to plan her next hit.

He could see the path leading away from the campsite and down to where they'd set up the start and finish points for the races. There was seating, kiosks, sponsored banners, and a photo booth, as well as a checkpoint that looked to be for the dogs.

Leblanc personally thought that the dogs adored to run and that their welfare was of the highest priority. They seemed like happy, contented animals, with an enviable life, but he was the first to admit that a psychopath with a need to kill never let facts get in the way of their agenda.

He paced down toward the finish point. Perhaps she would be here, looking for any signs of exhaustion in the dogs, collecting evidence to strengthen her resolve.

The blasts of whistles and the gathering of the crowds told Leblanc that a team was, in fact, heading for the finish line.

And at that moment, he glimpsed her. Without a doubt, this was the woman they were hunting.

Julia Marr was standing at the finish line, watching as the sled approached. He spotted the parka first, that distinctive pale blue, as he hurried toward her. She was a tall woman with broad shoulders. Dark hair curled from under her furry hat.

He could hear the group of dogs barking, hear the shouts and cheers of the racers. Julia stepped forward and Leblanc saw intent in every line of her body. He had a sudden, intense fear that she was going to try something now, that she was going to sabotage the incoming team, causing injury or worse.

"Julia Marr!" he shouted, as loud as he could.

She heard him. Her head jerked up. She turned away and rushed swiftly across the racetrack, ignoring the warning shouts of the officials.

Leblanc began running after her, but at that moment the shrill whistle of the race official sounded again.

"Stop, sir! Stop, please!" the yellow-jacketed official warned Leblanc, holding up a hand to stop him from crossing the racetrack and going in pursuit. Frustration surging, he had no choice but to comply.

A moment later, with a thundering of paws, the incoming dogs swept by, with the driver crouched in the sled, urging them on. Cheers erupted, and the dog musher fist-pumped the air as he reached the finish line. Leblanc waited, jogging from foot to foot, impatient for the sled to pass.

And then, checking there were no more incoming finishers, he ran across the snowy track, his adrenaline spiking. Would he catch up with her? Where had she gone?

There she was. She was in a knot of people much further down the hill. She was jogging purposefully away from him.

"Stop! Police!" he yelled. A few others looked curiously around.

But still she moved on, quickly, her head down, her shoulders hunched.

Leblanc felt his heart beating, hard and fast.

He saw her duck between some trees and he ran on to the point where she had disappeared from sight. She'd turned down one of the trails, a steep and winding descent into a narrow valley. There were some chalets further down, and some tents, amid a scattering of hillocks and boulders.

"Julia Marr!" he called again, scrambling down the trail after her. Where was she? There were several people around, clusters of visitors and racers. Leblanc looked frantically from side to side. She was gone!

And then, he realized with a shock, she wasn't.

Instead, she'd done something he hadn't anticipated at all. She'd removed her parka while in the cover of the crowds, and that had confused his eye. A black clad woman, dark hair streaming, was climbing up the rocky path and heading purposefully for the parking lot. She'd outwitted him, realized the blue was what he was looking for, and changed it.

"Police!"

Leblanc broke into a run, pounding toward the car lot, but fearing that he was going to be too slow and it would be too late. She was going to jump in a car and be gone before he could stop her.

55

CHAPTER TWELVE

Katie raced into the forest, hot in pursuit of the fleeing woman. Her footsteps thudded in her ears, soft and regular on the snowy path, but the trail wound so sharply that Katie could not see her.

It would be so easy for her to duck away onto a side track, to hide, to take one of the icy, rocky paths that wound into the trees, and to disappear for long enough that Katie lost her.

Time was not on their side. Especially since this woman knew that she was being chased.

If she got away, she could hide out and continue her deadly work, trying to chalk up as many kills as she could before they caught up again.

It was critical to catch her now.

Katie sped up, powering up the hill, the frigid air burning her lungs. On this well-trodden surface of chunky ice, fallen pine needles and drifting swathes of snow, she could not see fresh footprints clearly, and this increased the pressure to get this woman, fast, because the trail would be impossible to follow.

Katie dug deep and pushed harder, her breath bursting from her in steaming clouds. Her feet crunched through snow, her muscles ached.

But at least the woman was in sight. She caught a glimpse of her, silhouetted against a bright gap in the trees. And the woman saw her, too. She must have stopped to catch her breath, or else to check if she was still being followed, Katie thought. Glancing around, seeing Katie still in pursuit, she broke into a run and veered left, down a steep and icy trail.

Katie followed, her heart pounding, her breath burning in her chest. The trail was steep and slippery, with jutting roots and low, snow-covered branches. She ducked under them, snow cascading down.

And then, she stopped, surprised, because from ahead, she heard a terrified, breathless voice.

"Larry! Larry, can you hear me? Please, I need help! I'm being chased! I think this murderer is following me! I don't know how long I can keep going!"

Eyes widening, Katie stumbled to a breathless halt.

Was this woman referring to her?

"Er, I'm not a murderer," she called, in between gasps. "I'm an FBI agent! I need to question you."

There was a pause.

"Okay, Larry, hold on," the woman said. Now, pacing closer, Katie had her in sight. And now, with her hat askew and closer than she had been, she could see there were some differences from the woman in the photo.

This was not Julia Marr. She had a plumper face, and a rounder chin. The blue parka had pink trim, not red.

"How do I know you're an FBI agent?" the woman asked Katie suspiciously, chest heaving. She was holding a cellphone in her hand, from which a worried squawking was emitting.

"Here's my badge and ID." Katie showed her. "I needed to ask you questions, but you ran. Why did you run?"

"Because I was jumpy. You scared me."

"I yelled Police!" Katie protested.

"That's exactly what I'd yell, if I was a killer and I wanted someone to stop running," the woman replied, with some logic.

"What's your name?"

"Melissa Sudbury. I've been at the festival since yesterday. We camped out last night but we're going back home today. My boyfriend is out on a hike. He told me to be careful because this killer was around. Then you started yelling at me and I thought - well, I guess I thought my time had come."

She spoke into the phone again. "Larry, it's okay. This is an FBI agent. At any rate, I'm ninety-nine percent sure."

Ninety-nine percent? Katie felt slightly insulted that even after showing her official FBI credentials, there was still one percent of doubt in this woman's mind.

Melissa cut the call. "He's back from his hike, and coming to the trail head to find me."

"I'll walk with you," Katie said firmly. It was the least she could do, since she'd been the reason for this woman racing headlong into the woods. Now, she needed to make sure she got out again, and back with her partner, safely.

They trudged up the steep incline and back along the snowy trail.

"We're leaving a day early because of these murders," Melissa shared as they walked. "We don't want to spend another night out here. It's been fun, but now we don't feel it's safe."

"That's very wise," Katie said. She was glad that even if the festival organizers were digging in their heels, at least some members of the public were deciding for themselves it was safer to leave.

But this headlong pursuit had been a total waste of time, and now she was no closer to finding Julia Marr. She hoped Leblanc was having better success, and decided to check in with him as soon as she could. In the meantime, she'd need to resume the hunt.

They reached the trail head, in time to see a worried looking man in hiking gear hurrying up.

"This is Larry," Melissa said.

"Come on, babes. Let's get the tent packed up. I'm glad you were an FBI agent and not a killer," the young man said to Katie earnestly, before the two walked away, arm in arm.

Katie peeled off, not wanting to follow them any further, her mind whirring again as she assessed what direction she could take next, and where the real Julia Marr might be hiding.

She headed back the way she'd come, skirting the parking lot, deciding that she'd head into the training grounds and see if the animal rights activist was watching the teams at work.

But at that moment, she was aware of a commotion to her right. Movement caught her eye.

There was someone running - a woman in a fur hat. Katie clocked the scene instantly, twisting around to take it in. This black clad woman didn't fit her description - but that was because she was holding her jacket, scrunched up in her hand.

Looking further back, adrenaline now flooding her, Katie saw a familiar figure.

Leblanc was chasing this woman down, but he was too far away to catch her. Instantly, Katie saw this. The woman was heading into the roped-off parking area, making for a red SUV. Katie had to get to her before she climbed in.

She took off, racing toward the car from the opposite direction. This woman looked exactly like the picture, she realized. Her face was intent, her demeanor focused, and she was a darn fast runner.

And then, the woman noticed Katie. She glanced to her right, and saw she was being chased from the other direction. Her face twisted with fear, her expression desperate.

"Stop!" Katie yelled.

The woman didn't stop. And she must have had the car keys at the ready, because Katie saw the red SUV's lights flashing and knew she'd activated the central locking to open the doors. Now all she had to do was scramble in, start up, and speed away.

Katie put on a last burst of speed, her feet thudding over the packed snow. She had to stop this woman. It was imperative that she not get away. Her breath scorched her lungs.

She got just close enough to reach her. One chance was all she would have.

Katie made a leap for it and grabbed onto the hem of the woman's black jacket.

The effort knocked her off her feet, but she clung on tight, and the momentum pulled the woman down, too. She slipped and fell, sprawling onto the snow, yelling in outrage.

"How dare you do this? How dare you!" she shrieked, kicking and flailing. "Get off me! And get that jacket away from me. It has fur on the sleeves! Fur is murder!" She swatted at Katie's arm.

"FBI," Katie said breathlessly. "We need to question you. Regarding other murders. And I think this fur is fake, for what it's worth."

Keeping a tight grip on the struggling woman, Katie hauled her to her feet, holding her as best she could while Leblanc pounded up with the handcuffs.

They'd caught Julia Marr, but now the next challenge would be questioning her. Already, Katie could see that this woman had no respect for the law, and was ready to fight them every step of the way.

CHAPTER THIRTEEN

What would be the most effective way to question this troublemaker, Katie wondered. She decided that Julia Marr needed to be removed from the festival grounds, and from any semblance of her comfort zone. A neutral and official environment needed to be in place, so she decided that it would be better to interrogate her at the local RCMP department.

She'd tried to flee the police, she'd disobeyed a direct instruction to stop, and she'd turned into a fighting wildcat when Katie had brought her down. She had a scratch on her cheek from where Julia had attacked her. Undoubtedly, she was capable of violence. But had she taken that agenda further?

Was she capable of murder, to achieve the goals she was clearly intent on reaching?

"Let's take her in," she said to Leblanc, who nodded, understanding exactly why Katie was doing this.

With some difficulty, Leblanc got Julia into the back of the SUV. Even with her hands cuffed behind her, she was putting up a fight, and uttering a volley of abuse.

"Calm down," Leblanc ordered her through gritted teeth, fastening the seatbelt to secure the furious woman into place.

"How far away is the police department?" Katie asked, hoping it was close by. They hadn't even been there yet, since they'd driven straight to the festival grounds.

"Looks like a five-minute drive," Leblanc said.

Katie started up the car.

"You're going to regret this! I have a top legal firm on my side," Julia threatened from the back seat.

"Ms. Marr, we're questioning you in connection with the murders. That means we'll be asking you a few questions to confirm certain facts. If you're cleared when we're done, you will be free to go." Katie glowered into the rearview mirror.

"Oh, so now you think I'm a killer? Is this what you're doing to try and get me removed from site?"

"It's up to you to prove or disprove that."

Katie kept her voice calm as she sped along the main road toward the Soaring Crow RCMP department. It was in a somewhat lesser location than the festival organizer's office, tucked down a side road opposite a small self-storage warehouse.

It was getting dark and the fact that evening was setting in filled Katie with foreboding. If they didn't have the killer in the car - if Julia provided an alibi - they would be back to square one in the investigation, and nightfall seemed to be when the killer liked to hunt.

They parked outside the police department, and went through the process of getting Julia out of the car. She seemed to be resisting on principle now, Katie noted.

Leblanc practically dragged her along the well-swept path, and into the small police department, where a young, dark-haired, female officer at the front desk guiltily hid a half-eaten pretzel under the desk, looking surprised by their arrival.

"We need to use an interrogation room, please," Katie said, showing her badge. "We're working at the festival, investigating the killings."

"Sure. First door on the right. It's empty," the officer said, in a tone that told Katie that room was seldom, if ever, used.

The fact that this place was so peaceful, even during a big international festival, brought home to her again what a huge threat these murders represented. Not just to the victims, but to the town and its livelihood. She resolved that she was going to spend as long as it took to get the truth out of Julia. If they had to sit in that room till midnight or beyond, she was going to drill down into her movements and motives.

"I want my lawyer," Julia spluttered as they seated her behind the wooden table. Katie attached her handcuffs to the chair. "I'm being treated like a criminal here!"

"You're not charged with anything. Yet," Katie said, sitting opposite.

Julia snorted rudely.

"We are investigating murders, Ms. Marr. You are a person of interest because you've tried to sabotage the race in the past," Leblanc said. "You were at the finish line and it looked to me as if you were about to do the same thing again this time. So - how far are you taking this sabotage? All the way to murder?"

Julia tossed her head disdainfully. That took some nerve, in handcuffs, Katie decided.

"I was not intending to sabotage anything. I wanted to get a close-up video of the dogs. I wanted footage of their distress, and of the way the harness fit - or didn't fit."

"Can you prove that?" Leblanc said.

"It's obvious it didn't fit!"

Leblanc sighed. "I mean, can you prove your intention was to film?"

"I already have some footage. I began it when they approached. My phone's in my parka."

That was bundled up on the shelf. In this warm room, there was no need for outdoor clothing. Katie had taken her jacket off, too.

Katie uncuffed Julia so she could open the phone. Now that she'd calmed down some, she was willing to keep the cuffs off, for now, anyway.

She looked at the video footage and saw this was true. Julia had recorded an introduction, saying she was planning to film the dogs. She'd videoed the finish area and said that they were waiting for the first team to approach. So she had not been at the finish line intending to cause harm or sabotage while there. But now that she was talking, and looked willing to tell the truth, it was time to move onto her alibi for the times of the murders.

"There have been two people murdered at this festival. Did you know the victims?"

Julia shrugged. "I knew the young guy who sold the harnesses and equipment. I already spoke to him. I said that some of the items he sells use pain and force to subdue the animals and he should take them off his shelves. He laughed at me."

She made an angry face, and Katie raised internal eyebrows at this evidence of a personal motive.

"Can you account for your movements last night, and yesterday morning?" Katie said, remembering the times of the killings. The coroner had estimated that Thomas had been dead around twelve hours when his body was found, so he was killed at about seven or eight p.m., and Kevin had been dead about seven hours, so must have been killed in the early hours of that morning, just before dawn.

Julia sighed, as if she were already bored with the proceedings.

"Last night, I cooked some food and had an early night."

"Can anyone confirm that?"

"I was alone in the chalet. The other women - four of them - ate out. I don't like eating out as I'm not sure any of the places here offer a fully vegan option. I find it easier just to prepare food myself. So that's what I did. I made a vegetable stir fry, had a glass of wine, and was in bed by about nine p.m."

"Did you speak to anyone? Make any calls?"

She shook her head.

"How about early this morning?"

Now, Julia looked shifty. Her gaze slid away and Katie's focus sharpened.

"This morning I - er - I can't account for my movements."

"You realize that makes you a suspect, Ms. Marr? Why can't you account for your movements? Were you in the area of the kiosks?"

"No, I - I wasn't."

Again, Julia looked down.

Katie observed her, trying to work out what this change in her behavior meant. It meant something, that was certain, but she wasn't sure if it was what they were looking for.

She was a difficult suspect, she didn't want to talk, and she had an alternative agenda. But Katie suddenly wondered if that agenda was the reason why she was suddenly closing up again.

"Would there be any video footage that confirms your whereabouts at that time?" she asked, inspiration suddenly striking.

She picked up Julia's phone again.

"No!" The cry burst from Julia's lips. "That's - that's private stuff I've got on there!"

"This is a murder investigation," Katie said sternly.

She scrolled through the footage, and her eyes narrowed as she saw that there were several long videos, taken between five a.m. and seven a.m. this morning.

Leblanc leaned over as she played them.

The voice was Julia's, and the filming was being done in one of the dog runs. Without a doubt, Julia had sneaked in and filmed the conditions in which the dogs were kept. From the footage it looked as if she hadn't left until after it was light.

63

That was highly irregular, and Katie was not sure if it would be grounds for prosecution, based on the laws and the festival regulations. But it meant that her filming had provided her with a solid alibi for one of the murders. She could not have been hiding out in a dog run, and killing Kevin, at the same time.

"We're going to hand this over to the local RCMP," Katie told her sternly. "They can decide if they need to take action on this, so you'll be here a while longer. For now, though, you're cleared of murder."

She stood up and walked out, feeling suddenly tired. It had been a long day, and she'd had good hopes for this lead. Now, Julia - though acting illegally - was not their killer, and she had no other suspects who were even remotely on her radar.

And worse still, as she trailed out of the interrogation room and checked her phone, she saw that while she'd been battling with Julia's alibi, her mother had called.

She felt a pang of anxiety all over again, knowing Josie's unstable condition. Her mother would not just be checking in. She would have texted a general update. A call meant news. And at this point, news was unlikely to be good.

"I'll hand Julia over to the local RCMP, and update them," Leblanc said.

"While you do that, I'd better return this call," she said, walking quickly down the corridor to find a private place.

CHAPTER FOURTEEN

The most private place that Katie could find, without heading outside into the worsening wind, was a small utility room down the corridor from the interview room in the RCMP offices.

She hustled in, quickly taking the call, feeling a sense of dread that had started to be the norm with anything related to Josie.

"Mom, hi. Is everything okay?"

Waiting for her mother's reply, Katie breathed in the smell of polish and bleach. She wondered: will this be the place where I hear the news that means she'll never be all right? And then she realized to her alarm that she'd started to think this way every time her sister was discussed.

"Not really, Katie. Nothing's okay." Her mother stifled a sob. "We've just spoken to the doctor, and there's no change. No improvement in her condition."

"I'm so sorry. I know, it's like living through hell. If only Josie would respond to something," Katie said, knowing the comfort was empty but that it was all she had to offer.

"I know, I know. But what if she wants to, but can't?"

"What do you mean?" Katie asked, suddenly feeling trapped in the small room.

"I mean, what if she's in there, somewhere, wanting to come back to us, but she's just blocked herself from doing so, and her own mind or memory is making it impossible?"

"I guess that could be true," Katie said. If her mother was right, it didn't sound very positive, though.

"She doesn't even seem to hear us now. Maybe it's because she's so deeply sedated. The doctors - well, I don't know if they're going to have any answers." Her mother sighed. "I just don't know if she'll ever be the same again. I don't know if she'll ever be able to live anything like a normal life. Forgive me, Katie. Your dad doesn't know I'm calling. He got so upset yesterday when I said how hopeless I feel. He's trying to be so strong, so for him, I need to be, too. But I wanted you to know."

"I feel the same," Katie said softly.

"I had a dream last night that she came back. That she woke up, and she was okay. She was speaking, even, and I was so happy, because she was going to be better again. But then I woke up and realized it was just a dream." Her mother let out a sob.

Katie felt a deep ache inside. She exhaled, wanting to cry herself, to let out the pain that was building inside her, but at the same time knowing she needed to be strong for her mother.

"She's in the best place - getting the very best care. The equipment and medication is the top of the range, and the doctors are totally focused on her recovery." That was all she could default to.

"I guess so. At least we're getting a lot of support. People I don't even know, at the hospital, are asking if there's anything they can do. We've been given restaurant vouchers for ourselves, body products for Josie that are supposed to soothe and calm. Everyone's being so kind. I keep thinking something has to work eventually if we keep having faith. But the doctor says we're out of time. So right now - well, Katie, if she's still the same by tomorrow evening, I think we're going to have to go ahead with the electrotherapy."

"You think?" Katie's sense of doom was worsening now. Her mother thought that?

"It's the only thing that looks like it will work. I've been preparing myself for it. That she'll be changed, she'll never be the same, but at least she'll be calmer. At least she'll be - manageable, I guess."

Katie shook her head. The idea of that therapy still filled her with a sick horror. But maybe her mother was right, and she needed to put her own feelings aside and do what was best for Josie.

"I'll think about it with an open mind," she promised. "And I'll let you know tomorrow evening. If I'm still on the case here, I'll call you. But if I get the chance, and this is wrapped up before then, I'll fly back. Take care, Mom."

"And you, Katie. Be careful."

Her mother cut the call, and Katie hurried back to the lobby, feeling somber.

Leblanc was on the phone, pacing up and down. He finished the call, and turned to Katie.

"As you can imagine, accommodation here is at a premium. I didn't think we were going to find anywhere, but I've managed to organize something. Luckily, a few guests have been checking out early because of the killings."

Katie nodded, remembering her own experience earlier today with the false lead she'd followed.

"The more people who leave, the better," she said somberly.

"There's a small hotel right on the edge of the festival grounds, that has two rooms available. It's called Betelgeuse Place. I've booked us in. I think we should head there now," he said, checking his watch.

Katie pressed her lips together, feeling defeated. Leblanc was right. Things were winding down. With the intense cold, and the wind that seemed to worsen at night, there weren't many activities that took place after dark, and she could already see the main street was quiet.

"Let's check in," she said, bringing up the map on her phone to orient herself.

She stepped out of the police department, and was hit by a blast of cold air. Shivering, she pulled her jacket around her tightly. The wind was picking up strongly, and she could see that clouds were moving in.

"Do you think it could be one of the racers?" she asked, as they hurried to the car.

"One of the racers?"

"I was thinking, when I was watching the activity in the organizer's office earlier, how invested these racers are in the outcome. Perhaps someone is killing people because he didn't win, or because there was a problem with his race. Perhaps he thinks that certain people, somehow, deserved to die because of that. It could be why he now wants to kill random people, and sabotage the festival."

If a psychopath was taking part in the race, the need for revenge might be something that seemed logical to him. And psychopaths could be found in all walks of life.

"That's definitely something to consider," Leblanc said.

"You don't think it's a good theory?" Feeling stressed and angry after the debacle of her sister, Katie was now annoyed that she could hear doubt in Leblanc's voice.

"I do think it's a good theory," Leblanc said, now sounding equally annoyed. "I'm thinking about it, that's all."

"You sounded like you were discarding it!" Katie retorted.

"I was wondering if it was logistically possible. As the racers, or dog mushers as I think they are called, are mostly out on races at the moment. They wouldn't have had time to do this," Leblanc said.

"They're not all out! There are many different lengths of race. Don't you remember what we were told? Some of the sprint races are just happening tomorrow."

"Well, then it's an excellent theory. Let's go out and question them all, immediately." Sarcasm dripped from his voice.

Katie forced herself not to snap back, and to take a few deep breaths. She still felt too emotional to be able to hold a normal conversation. She was making Leblanc angry, getting under his skin. And he was doing the same to her. It was because they were both tired, both frustrated, and after a long, cold day they had made no progress whatsoever.

They parked outside the hotel, which was a two-story building made of solid wood, with a row of small pine trees outside, threaded with colored lights that gave it a Christmas card charm.

Still not speaking to her, Leblanc stomped inside.

The receptionist nodded a greeting.

"Good evening," she said. "Here are your room keys. Yours is on the first floor, ma'am, and yours on the second floor, sir. There's a kitchen on the first floor where we have a variety of drinks and snacks - sodas, sandwiches, and the like. Those are included in the rate. Let me know if you need anything extra."

"Thanks," Katie said.

She took her key, and stomped off to her room.

It smelled fragrantly of wood, and there was a fire burning in the small fireplace. The bed was wedged into one corner, and behind a wall was a tiny bathroom with a shower. It was cozy and it was warm.

But even after unpacking her toiletries and having a quick shower, Katie didn't feel tired.

She felt restless and grumpy. Even though they'd just gotten under each other's skin, she found she was missing Leblanc. Taking separate rooms felt wrong after the closeness they'd shared. And they hadn't had a chance to apologize to each other for the fight. They would have, if they'd had the same room.

Briefly she considered walking upstairs and knocking on his door to smooth things over, but decided against it.

She didn't want him to think she was knocking for other reasons. Things didn't need to be more complicated than they already were. She'd apologize first thing tomorrow.

Then another thought occurred to her, that if the killer was out there, he might be using this quiet time, and the cold, icy dark to do his work.

She felt sure that he would be out there, and that he was going ahead with his plans.

Maybe, if she went out now, she could get an insight into what he was doing, and learn more about him, she reasoned. It would be freezing, but if he could operate in these harsh conditions, so could she.

She pulled on her boots and parka, suddenly feeling desperate to get out, to feel the snow under her boots, to try and achieve some peace and balance in her mind.

She'd need to be careful though, she reminded herself, as she eased the hotel door open and stepped outside. It wasn't safe here anymore and there was a reason why people had left.

In this icy night, the murderer could be on the hunt - and could perceive her as a threat, or else a target.

CHAPTER FIFTEEN

Charley Kaye trudged over the grounds, carrying a trash bag and a pointed stick to pick up those smaller items of rubbish that his thick gloves couldn't grasp, as well as a shovel.

Usually he worked in a team, with a partner, but his partner was off sick with bronchitis and that meant twenty-one-year-old Charley was on his own. Well, not on his own. There were other cleaners in the vicinity; there was a group of them. But everyone except him was working as a pair because the organizers had told them to.

For some reason, as he walked slowly around the area tonight, he felt uneasy. As if someone might be watching him.

Charley had an instinct that way, he always knew if there were eyes on him, and right now he definitely felt it. Perhaps it was because of these murders that were spooking everyone, but he felt something was wrong. It was much quieter tonight than usual, although that could be because it was also colder. But he thought people were scared.

He stopped for a moment, looked around, but there was nothing to be seen. He blinked fast, his blue eyes watering in the cold.

With the wind picking up, it was difficult to tell. Trees were rustling, tents were swaying, flags and banners were flapping. There was a lot of movement around.

Forcing his mind back to the job and away from that strange, scared place where it had briefly strayed, he set off in pursuit of a fluttering napkin, trapping it with his stick.

Cleaning up after visitors who had been out and about all day was definitely not the most glamorous job. There was always a lot of litter at these events.

He supposed folks felt that it was the acceptable thing to do, to litter while they were enjoying themselves. People were bad that way, disgusting, actually. They had no thought or care for their environment, relying on someone else to gather up their soda cans and burger wrappers, their discarded Kleenexes and event tickets.

Sometimes, people even left behind items of value. Good gloves, purses. Charley was an honest man and he always took these to lost property. Only if there was random cash, coins discarded on the ground with no purse and no owner, would he keep it for himself. That was fair, right? He always made a few dollars extra that way over this time.

But the trash pickup was only one part of his job. There was another, even bigger job he had, and that was to clean up after the dogs.

It was supposed to be the job of the handlers, the mushers, but they didn't do it, of course.

He'd already collected a whole bag of frozen dog poop. It was essential to clear this from the area. People didn't like it and they complained like crazy if they stepped in it or got it on their shoes.

Despite the fact that this was, after all, a dog sled festival. Charley thought that was quite funny. It made him laugh at the illogicality of it.

Actually, the dogs themselves he enjoyed the most. He had a real affinity with animals. He'd always liked them. The dogs were interesting. He liked the way they snuffled and ran around, their tails wagging, the way they interacted, the way they seemed to run in a pack. And he liked how naughty these dogs were. Real naughty, rebellious dogs. If they got loose from their handlers, they'd just run, as far and fast as they could, just for the sheer joy of it. The commotion this inevitably caused was always a laugh.

Everyone found it so, except for the handlers, who tended to lose their sense of humor when it was their personal dog heading for the hills.

Charley looked up sharply, his thoughts suddenly interrupted.

Had that been a movement? Behind that kiosk? He thought for sure he'd seen something.

The organizers had told him to be careful and that he must keep the local police on speed dial and call them immediately if he heard or saw anything unusual, or if he was worried.

He was worried now, but he didn't know why.

It was more a feeling. A tingling, creepy sense that things weren't right. He couldn't put his finger on why.

The hairs on the back of his neck were prickling and it felt as if he was being watched. For a moment, he thought whoever had been there had gone, but then he heard the slight crunch of a footstep. Or, at any rate, he thought it was that.

Perhaps it was nothing. Perhaps he was just being too sensitive. Perhaps a dog had run off and a handler was crashing through the woods in pursuit, although he heard no calls or whistles.

At any rate, he couldn't call the police for nothing. Charley didn't even like the police. He didn't trust them.

He turned his head, looked back over his shoulder at the rows of booths, tents and stalls that lined the ice. Charley frowned, trying to locate the sound again. There was nothing to see but the eerie light of the moon and the strong wind that made the flags and banners dance.

He couldn't determine if there was someone behind him or if it was closer to him.

"Hey! Anyone there?" he called, but the wind snatched his words away. Not even the cleaning team in the distance, two people working on the other side of the race finish line, heard him.

He looked back at the fences and out over the seemingly endless snow-covered fields beyond. Even in this light, he could see the dark shadowy forms of trees.

He saw nothing apart from that. Or rather, no one. But that didn't mean no one was there.

The wind was directly in his face, making it hard to hear anything, but he was getting so spooked that now, he was considering going over to join the team of two he could see in the distance, and ask if he could work with them because it felt safer.

Maybe that would be the best idea. He'd look stupid if he called the police. They'd just think he was making it up. He must be getting jumpy, frightened. It was all to do with these murders, wasn't it?

But even so, Charley decided to check the woods. He resolved to stop what he was doing, walk around and make sure there was no one hiding anywhere. He wasn't afraid of anyone, he told himself. But he did want to make sure.

He dropped his bag and the trash stick, picked up the shovel with both hands and began to walk slowly towards the trees.

The wind was now stronger, gusting viciously, pummeling his parka, whipping tears from his eyes.

The longer he walked, the more certain he was that his instincts were right. It was looking as if there was someone crouched down among the fallen logs by the trees.

Charley walked closer and closer to the trees, which now seemed to loom over him. He felt suddenly cold, and realized that the moon wasn't giving him enough light to see by.

The shadows were getting darker and darker.

"If you're there, come out!" he threatened.

But there was no reply and no movement. Finally, he got close enough to see clearly.

He let out a huge sigh of relief. It wasn't a person. It was a discarded backpack, in pink and white, that had looked a lot like flesh color from a distance. Some kid must have forgotten it. He'd take it to lost property.

He picked it up, feeling relieved, and headed back.

But the next moment, Charley's legs were cut from under him and he sprawled onto the ground, letting out a terrified yell, his heart racing.

Someone had been waiting for him, someone was going to get him. He cowered down, his breath coming harshly.

And then, slowly, he scrambled to his feet, piecing together what had happened.

He'd stumbled over something. He hadn't been pushed or shoved. He'd just come across a sudden, large, solid obstruction in the soft snow and it had knocked him right off his feet.

Staring down, Charley saw what it was that had tripped him up.

And, as he stared into the unseeing eyes, the sheet white face, and saw the gaping slash in the neck, the red-stained snow, terror overcame him – the mortal terror of acknowledging that there was someone out here, someone close by, who was killing in this brutal way.

Panicked, Charley yelled even louder.

"Help! There's another one! Help, help, come quick!" He backed away, hugging himself, staring around as fear consumed him, wondering where this killer was, whether he'd gone away.

Or whether he was still nearby, and waiting.

CHAPTER SIXTEEN

Katie kept on walking more through sheer stubbornness than anything else, she acknowledged, ducking her head against the persistent, worsening wind. Coming out at night had been a stupid idea, but right now, she was all out of good ideas. In a way she thought she deserved the blast of cold air that scoured her to the bone. At least it might prompt a rush of blood to the brain.

For now, though, she found herself obsessed with Leblanc, fretting about the decisions she'd made, remembering the moments they'd shared together, their intimacy, and the way his eyes softened when he smiled. It left her unable to focus on the case.

She also felt strangely spooked. The blasts of icy air caused trees to sway and leaves to flutter, and as she forged forward, Katie found herself constantly looking over her shoulder, believing she saw someone out of the corner of her eye.

She knew she had to be careful, because out here in the cold she was an observer, but could also be a target. And with this wind howling, it was difficult to hear the subtle sounds that might mean someone was sneaking up on her.

Weirdly, even though she was out in the open, Katie decided that the sounds and movements of this wind made her feel claustrophobic.

As she trudged through the snow, she wondered if this would mean bad weather would interfere with the start of the main festival tomorrow.

That might be good, she acknowledged. Anything that shut things down would be helpful. She had a sick feeling inside that the killer was still ahead of them, still planning his strikes, still pursuing his agenda without any fear of being caught.

And then, over the howling of the wind, Katie did hear something, and her head jerked to the right.

A terrified yell came from the forest border, near the festival grounds.

"Help, there's another one! Help, help, come quick!"

Gasping in a tense breath, Katie ran for it, sprinting toward the cries. This was the sound of genuine fear. It was the sound of someone who was staring down at a dead body. She knew this immediately, instinctively. This was no false alarm. He'd struck again, perhaps even killed while she was out here fighting this blisteringly cold wind.

She pounded through the snow. Others were running, too. She hadn't even known there were people out on the grounds at this time, but as she saw figures in yellow vests and green parkas rush across the snow, she now realized that the clean-up crew must be working after closing time.

She saw the source of the cries. A young, stocky man, clutching a pink and white backpack and a shovel was staring down into the snow. He looked paralyzed with terror, and before Katie even reached him, she knew with a sense of finality what she would see.

"It's - it's a dead person. There's a man here who's been murdered. I – I can't believe this is happening," the man said, casting her a terrified glance and backing away another few steps.

Two of the crew ran up and stopped in their tracks, staring at the body, wide-eyed and mouths agape. They were obviously in shock.

"Step back, step back," Katie said, trying for calmness. She needed to manage the situation, and fast. There might be evidence, footprints, something they could use, and the scene needed to remain undisturbed - as far as possible. "Call the police, someone, please. And stay well away from it, and over to the side here."

This was especially important since it looked to be recent. The man staring up at her, wide-eyed, pale-faced, with his throat slashed, could not have been here long.

This body could not have been dumped today, or it would have been discovered. It was right on the border of the festival grounds. She'd seen people walking here just a couple of hours ago.

This was a fresh kill, Katie realized with a chill.

Stepping forward, making sure to plant her feet squarely in the prints the cleaner had already made, she bent down, removed her own glove, and touched the man's hand, noticing that he was not wearing gloves. What did that mean? Had the killer removed them, or had this man been snatched from an indoor location?

She could detect no rigor mortis, and in fact, thought she could feel a residual warmth. The knowledge that this was so recent made her feel sick.

The killer had been here. Right here. He'd planted this body and delivered the slash to the throat confidently and boldly, not worried about being seen or discovered.

He was arrogant, that was for sure. Reckless perhaps, but they were still lagging far behind, because he had made a kill literally under their noses. Standing up, she scanned the woods, looking for any sign that he might be hiding, or else waiting around to enjoy the sensation he'd caused.

Was he doing this just to cause a commotion and terrify people? Or was there another reason, and if so what was it?

She felt a flash of frustration that they were not fully able to understand his motives. If they understood why he was leaving the bodies here, and what he really wanted to achieve, Katie had no doubt at all that the information would lead straight to the killer.

Was he watching? Was it important to him to see the scene play out?

But apart from a multitude of rustling leaves and branches, she could see no obvious sign of anyone in the woods. Even so, this had been too close for comfort. It hadn't been safe going out. But nor was it safe for the cleaners to work. And the fact that this man seemed to have been taken while inside was also troubling as it meant the killer was not simply picking victims from among the crowds.

Worst of all, they had been too slow. She hadn't been able to stop him, a truth that burned her.

Already, she could hear the shrilling of sirens as the local police arrived at the festival grounds. It was time to break the bad news to her partner. Katie got out her phone and called Leblanc.

He answered within one ring.

"What is it, Katie?" His voice was tense. He feared the worst.

"Another victim, near the camping grounds at the south of the site," she said tersely. "You'll see it when you step outside."

"I'll be there now." He hung up.

The police were arriving, three officers, with a coroner's van not far behind. Katie was grateful for their quick response. This scene needed to be roped off and managed, as fast as possible.

Katie stepped back from the scene, and hurried over to the witness who'd found the body, wanting to get an eyewitness account while the scene was still fresh in his mind. The festival grounds cleaner was sitting in the snow now, looking pale and nauseous.

"What happened?" Katie said gently. "Do you feel ready to speak about it?"

"I – sure. I guess I am. But there's not much to say," he said, staring at her with a stricken expression. "I had this weird feeling. I was sure there was someone watching me. I - I had that instinct, you know?"

Katie nodded. "Yes, I know."

"I went to try and see what it was. I found this in the snow nearby." He indicated the backpack lying on the snow. "And then, I stumbled over that man, literally fell over him. He was lying in the snow, covered with it."

"Was the backpack near him?" Katie asked, wondering if it had been in this man's possession, even though it looked more like an item that a girl would carry.

"No. It was probably ten yards away, by the logs over there. I thought maybe - maybe someone had sat down and forgotten it. It often happens. Most nights, we pick up something that's been left. That's the reason I went over there and then, I found him."

So the backpack was a coincidence, and the body had been roughly covered in snow, enough that it had been camouflaged from a casual glance. It had been unlucky he'd been found tonight and Katie now wondered if the killer had assumed that his latest victim would only be found in the morning. Or perhaps he hadn't cared, and had just wanted to make sure by dumping it on the festival grounds that it would be found at some point.

Katie recalled that all the bodies had been covered. Not buried, but simply covered over with a thin blanket of snow. She didn't know if this meant anything, or why the killer was doing it. Perhaps it had some sort of significance to him.

"We don't have an ID on this victim," one of the police called, and Katie looked around sharply. This was not going to be helpful.

"Someone must know him, if he's from here. Get a photo, send it in, see if anyone recognizes him," the other officer said.

"What if he's a tourist?" another police officer asked.

"We'll deal with that disaster if it happens," the first one said, his voice hard.

At that moment, Katie saw that Leblanc had arrived. His face looked set and stern. She had the strong feeling he'd also been unable to sleep, and had been lying awake, thinking, and worrying, just as she'd been doing.

"This is the worst case scenario," he said quietly, leaning close to her to be heard over the commotion of voices and the whistling wind.

"I know. They need to call off this event," Katie said.

"We can ask them again. But they won't. They're hell bent on finishing it. They'll complain it will be logistically impossible," Leblanc said.

"Even so, I'm going to keep telling them," Katie stated. "I'm going to talk to Pope again as soon as I can. Surely, he must realize."

At that moment, over the crackle of radios nearby, Katie picked up that there was some news on the victim's ID.

"One of the other guys knows him," an RCMP officer said, and Katie's ears pricked up.

"Who is he?" she asked, moving toward him.

"He's a lawyer. Mr. Menzies. He lives in town. Works in the office park across the road from the police department."

A lawyer? Had he been taken while at the office, or at home? And why him?

"Was he connected with the festival or the race at all?" she asked.

The officer got on the radio again. He spoke, listened, spoke again, and then turned back to her.

"My colleague doesn't think so, and he knows who's who. Menzies is definitely not one of the organizers this year, or on a committee, as he says he's met with all of them."

He spoke into the radio again. "He says Mr. Menzies does most of the legal work for the town. He's the go-to person for everything from contracts to suing people. Or he was, rather." The officer glanced, horrified, at the gory scene.

"Thanks," Katie said. She moved away, walking in step with Leblanc.

"I'm thinking we need to explore your theory urgently," Leblanc said.

"My theory?" Katie asked, surprised.

"Yes. Your theory that it might be a disgruntled racer, someone who was in trouble in the past. Because this latest victim wasn't involved in the festival. He was a lawyer. So perhaps this killer is looking at a scenario from last year. Taking revenge on a previous group of people that he perceives as having wronged him somehow. Maybe one of the racers did something wrong, and was sued, or even banned. That would make this a revenge move, right? Maybe the lawyer played a part in that, and he was killed for revenge, while the others were just chosen to create fear."

That theory made sense, to Katie.

"Let's go and check out that possibility, right now," she agreed.

CHAPTER SEVENTEEN

For this new direction, Katie knew they were going to need the help of the race organizer, as well as the local police. They needed to use all the resources they could to track down the records of historic races, and any trainers or dog mushers who'd caused trouble in the past.

They had the race organizer's business card, but when she dialed Mr. Pope's personal cellphone, she found it busy.

That was not surprising, Katie thought. By now, Pope would know what had happened and she was sure he was desperately involved in doing damage control. She doubted he was going to have time to call back. She wondered if she should try Jason, his likeable older brother, but then remembered Jason was not involved in the organization.

That left the local police - who were also clearly stretched to their limits, with some of the RCMP officers on the scene, and others, she saw, being deployed in security patrols.

Soaring Crow's community was rallying all its resources to help the town combat this deadly threat.

"I guess we might get lucky if we actually go to the police department," Leblanc said, looking around at the organized chaos, and drawing the same conclusions that Katie was busy doing.

"I think it's going to be the only way," she agreed. "They will have someone there manning the office."

Checking the time, she saw it was now after midnight. It was going to be a long, tough night for the police out on patrol, with the temperature plummeting, and the chances of finding the killer growing smaller with every passing minute. By now, Katie was sure, he was back in bed, and most probably laughing at the thought of the mayhem he'd caused. She felt a flare of actual hatred for someone who could act in this cold, callous way as if only his own agenda mattered. What a towering ego it took. She felt furiously intent that they were going to bring this man down.

Police were already tracking the prints, but Katie could see that in the trodden snow, the mass of footprints left after the day's festival were little more than slight indentations. Fresh snow would have offered a canvas for better footprints, but they hadn't been so lucky.

Perhaps the angle she and Leblanc were taking would produce results.

Katie headed back to the hotel and climbed into the car. She and Leblanc drove the short distance back to the RCMP offices, with the car buffeted by wind on the road. There, a gray-haired, capable looking officer was the only man on site.

"Are you here to do some research?" he asked on seeing the two of them. "I'm Officer Flannery. What can I help you with? Whatever it is, let's get this guy behind bars."

He frowned angrily, clearly as mad as Katie was that the town's festival was being destroyed by a rogue killer who'd struck yet again.

"We need access to your records and databases," Katie said. "Also, someone with local knowledge would be helpful."

She looked inquiringly at him, and he nodded. "If it's local knowledge, I can help. I've been working here, and with the festival, for years."

"That really will be a help," Katie said gratefully.

The nonstop ringing phone and crackling radio were going to be an issue, she guessed, but Officer Flannery brought both into the side annex, just off the main lobby, so he could keep an eye out for anyone coming in.

He settled them into the small room, which was a cross between an office space and a refreshment area. It had a table, a small kitchenette, and a refrigerator. He carried a laptop through and set it up.

"This is connected to the local databases," he said, glancing through to the lobby, which for now, seemed quiet.

Then the phone rang, and Katie waited patiently while he took the call.

"We have police patrolling throughout the night, ma'am," Flannery said. "We would advise everyone to stay indoors, and if you do need to step outside, do not go alone. We're hoping an arrest will be made very soon."

He glanced at Katie and Leblanc with a slightly cynical air, as if to emphasize that he knew an arrest was not imminent, but nonetheless he was hoping.

"We need to look through your records to see if there are any incidents from the festival for previous years," Katie said, once

81

Flannery had cut the call. "In particular, we want to know if one of the racers, or the dog mushers, got into trouble for any reason."

"You think this might be some kind of revenge move?" Flannery asked, picking up immediately on Katie's train of thought.

"That's what we're wondering, yes."

"We keep an incident book relating to each festival. Everything that gets called in, we record in there. That's so that we can improve our policing in the following years."

Katie thought that sounded like positive news for them. "So even if it doesn't result in charges being pressed, it still goes into the book?" she asked.

"That's correct. Also, we do have a few official charges from every event. There are always some incidents that go too far, and end up being actual offenses, and we're strict on those. No free passes for festival goers - this is a law abiding town," Flannery said solemnly.

Katie knew that this attitude, while being essential for effective policing, probably caused clashes with the organizers.

Suddenly, she felt glad they had ended up coming here first, as they might well get a more complete account from the police than they would from the organizer, whose vested interests might lead to downplaying bad behavior.

"I'm going to take a look back through the online case records. You're welcome to look with me, or go through the book." Flannery turned to the laptop and powered it up.

"I'll look with you, if Katie wants to go through the book," Leblanc offered.

While the laptop was connecting to the local databases, Flannery went through to the back office. He returned with an actual hard-cover notebook.

"Some of the handwriting is not great," he admitted to Katie. "Seems like we have a few on the team who should have become doctors, rather than gone into policing."

She gave a quick grin, glad of his humor, lightening the mood at this tough time.

And then they all got down to work.

For the next while, Katie knew she had to concentrate on keeping her eyes on the pages of the notebook, and not let her mind stray to the terrible events of the night.

The offenses were varied. A few of the festival guests had simply been drunk, resulting in fights and minor damage to property. Breakages, accidental falls, and conflict that didn't result in any serious injuries all seemed to have been recorded in the book, without charges being laid. There were several incidents of falls on the ice, some reports of missing property, and one incident of a home invasion which raised Katie's eyebrows until she saw that in the dark, a rather drunk visitor had simply gone into the wrong chalet and made himself at home there until the occupants woke up.

Then, in addition to those very minor incidents, there were more serious ones. There were a couple of genuine burglaries and a few incidents of pickpocketing and cellphone theft. Most of these remained unsolved - fairly typical for a big, outdoor event in an area with no cameras and with scarce police resources.

There was one accusation that caught Katie's eye, and she guessed it must have been taken further.

It was an incident of assault.

One of the dog mushers, Ed Knowles, had assaulted a visitor who'd come up to him and started inquiring about whether he'd cheated in the race. Mr. Knowles had responded angrily and it had quickly escalated into a fight. Being late at night and after the race, Katie guessed that at least one party, and probably both, had too much to drink. It looked as if the visitor had in fact made charges, although they had since been dropped.

"Leblanc, Flannery," she said quickly. They both looked up.

"This is the first incident that I've found that involves a racer. It's a charge of assault. It was dropped. I'd like to know why, and what the outcome was."

She turned the book so that they could read.

Flannery nodded. "Yes. I remember that well. It was a very unpleasant incident. Both men were drunk, but Ed Knowles was to blame. He handled it very badly and he got violent. He ended up punching the victim, Barry Snaith, several times, and in fact he ended up getting him on the floor. He knocked his head, he was bruised, and I think he broke his phone."

"Why wasn't it taken further?" Katie asked.

"The festival organizers stepped in and tried to resolve the situation. I think in the end, Knowles paid for a new phone, for the doctor's bill, and for the 'pain and suffering' in a private deal. If I remember, Snaith was flying back home to Michigan the next day and didn't want to delay his flight or get caught up in a police case. It wasn't ideal. We didn't feel that it had been appropriately handled by a lawyer, and not by the RCMP." He shrugged.

"A lawyer?" Was this a link, she wondered.

"I don't know which lawyer," he admitted. "Menzies was the go-to lawyer for this sort of case, though."

"Were there any further consequences?" Katie asked.

"Ed Knowles did get a lifetime ban. The organizers said he's not allowed to compete at this event again, ever."

"Is that so?"

Katie and Leblanc exchanged an excited glance. This was getting somewhere, at last. There was a real reason for Ed Knowles, who was clearly a violent man, to have big issues with the festival.

The next, and most important question was one Katie was ready to ask.

"Where does Ed Knowles live?"

Flannery pressed more keys.

"I don't think he's very local, but I do think he lives in the wider area," he said thoughtfully. "Yes, that's right. He lives on a big farm, about fifty miles out of town. If I remember, he is also a small time breeder of Alaskan Malamutes. That, he still does, even though he can no longer race."

Katie stood up, pushing her chair back.

"Thank you very much for the information," she said, writing down the address. "We'll go and see him now."

Flannery shook his head. "Don't go now. It's a long drive, and with this wind getting stronger by the minute, and icy roads, it's going to be dangerous. The wind is set to peak at around midnight, and die down in the small hours."

"We'll wait till morning," she said reluctantly. Presumably, if Knowles was the killer, he might have sped home ahead of the worsening wind – or else, he was also holed up somewhere for now.

Katie resolved that at sunrise tomorrow, she was going to be on Knowles's doorstep, asking questions.

She hoped his answers would be worth the wait.

CHAPTER EIGHTEEN

Katie gripped the wheel, staring out at the icy, still-dark road in front of her. It was early morning - just past six a.m., and after a few hours of fractured sleep, they were finally on the road.

The drive to Ed Knowles's house had taken more than an hour, and they were now close to their destination. She felt hopeful that in a few more minutes they would be face to face with their killer.

A disgruntled dog musher taking revenge would account for the fact that the town's lawyer, with no connection to the race, had been chosen as the most recent victim. The lawyer could have handled the legal issues between Ed Knowles and the race organizers. And thus, he could have been targeted. As for the other victims, perhaps they were a smokescreen. Or perhaps the racer was simply intent on causing as much collateral damage as he could.

The scenery was getting bleaker and bleaker as they drove, and Katie noted that the weather was definitely closing in. Clouds were gathering, dark and forbidding.

"Looks like snow, maybe tonight," Leblanc said.

"Maybe," Katie agreed. "But it could blow over."

Neither of them spoke about the possibility of the snow canceling the festival, and Katie knew that this was because they were both hoping they were on the way to the correct suspect.

If they could catch the killer first thing this morning, then the festival could go ahead. It would be a success and people would be safe.

But Katie didn't want to think about the consequences if things didn't turn out this way. She was sure that Leblanc, also, was keeping firmly away from that line of thought right now.

At least things were back to normal between them. The friction from last night was gone. Katie felt short on sleep and stressed to the nines in every direction, but at least there was now harmony once again between herself and her partner.

Working together, they could solve this. She felt sure of it.

Katie was now convinced that Ed Knowles was a man with a lot of issues. His violent behavior had played out once before, and Katie wondered if it could have escalated again.

She glanced at the map, wondering how the line of the road in the image could bear so little resemblance to the faded, pitted blacktop, with huge potholes and areas of complete erosion, that stretched before her now.

"This is a tough country," Leblanc observed.

Katie nodded agreement. Without a doubt, this far north, the freezing temperatures and inhospitable surroundings bred an equally hard type of person.

Ed Knowles was a violent man, who'd assaulted a person and who was clearly someone who lived by his own rules. Katie knew that she and Leblanc would need to be cautious and on their guard. They would have to be ready to contain his violence, and ready to defuse the situation if it threatened to explode.

Going into this kind of confrontation, Katie had no illusions about the risks.

The sun was starting to rise now, peeking from a gap in the clouds in a fiery burst of orange and gold, before being swallowed up by them again and providing a gray, muted daylight. From within the car she could feel the wind was still strong, with the car shuddering as it drove, though it had died down from the gale force blast last night.

And there, ahead of them, the map was telling them they had reached their destination. Even so, she felt amazed that there could be any end points on a road that felt as if it ran into the depths of nowhere.

But at last, ahead was a craggy driveway that stretched up into snow covered hills. An old wire gate was closed. Leblanc climbed out and half carried, half pushed it open. Katie drove through, and Leblanc closed it again before climbing back in.

"Damned cold out there," he observed, shivering, as Katie eased the car up the rocky trail.

They skirted a snow covered hillock and drove over a small bridge that was totally iced over. And then ahead, beyond a grove of pines, she saw the house.

It was an old farmhouse, with a sloping, snow covered roof, peeling walls, and a green-painted front door that Katie thought looked due for a touch-up. There was a porch, with a dilapidated swing, and a well-worn path leading to the front door.

Behind the house, she saw a large barn, and a couple of smaller buildings. Those looked to be in better condition than the house, she thought.

She rolled the car to a halt, very aware that the place felt creepy, and with a distinct atmosphere of abandonment. Then, she and Leblanc climbed out of the car.

It was eerily still - there was no sign of life in this snowy scene. Was he even home? Or was he still at the festival, laying low, waiting for a chance to kill again?

There hadn't been a cellphone registered in his name or they could at least have called it, even if tracking wouldn't be possible this far out in the wild.

As she walked towards the front door, Katie felt her heart pounding. She knew that anything could happen here. And that was what she was prepared for. The worst case scenario would be that Knowles wasn't here. But in that case they could always ask one of the local police to wait here, and arrest him when he did come home. And they could then return to the festival to hunt for him.

The only other solution was that he'd gone elsewhere to hide out, thinking a jump ahead of the police. That would be a complication. But first things first.

"Well, I guess we'll find out if he's here now," she said.

"You want to take a look around first?" Leblanc asked, glancing uneasily around the quiet, gloomy farm, clearly feeling as on edge as Katie.

She thought that over, but then shook her head.

"We don't want to end up snooping, or trespassing. Not with a man like this. If he sees us, he could aim a shotgun out of a window and pull the trigger. From his behavior that seems to be the kind of man he is."

Leblanc nodded, his hand moving to his own gun. He eased off his thick glove, flexing his fingers in the bitter cold as he closed his hand over the grip.

"Better to knock, and give him warning then," he agreed.

Katie raised her hand and grasped the brass knocker on the front door. She brought it down with a bang.

The sound resounded around them and for a few moments, Katie wondered if this place really was empty, and if Knowles wasn't here at all. Maybe he'd moved out or was hiding out.

But then, she heard the clear, sharp noise of a dog barking from somewhere behind the house.

It was soon joined by more barks. A chorus, a volley of barks. A clamor of canine voices that sounded as if an entire pack was heading their way. Suddenly, the threatening quiet was shattered.

Katie glanced at Leblanc, feeling worried now.

She had no doubt that these animals would be dangerous, and that the prospect of facing them was not pleasant. She knew that any dog that was let loose and feeling protective of its territory was capable of surprising aggression and attack. And this was not just one or two dogs, but many.

"Maybe we should wait in the car," she said, as the sound of barking completely filled the air. She turned away from the front door, but realized to her consternation that this was no longer possible, because they were all out of time.

With an angry snarling and yelping, a pack of at least twelve fierce looking dogs rounded the house. Seeing Katie and Leblanc standing outside the front door, the barking increased in pitch as the pack raced to where Katie and Leblanc were standing.

She didn't see one Alaskan Malamute in the throng of mixed dogs that were racing up, which confused her, since Knowles was a breeder of them. She saw dogs of all other shapes and sizes. Some huge. A gigantic Great Dane stood practically eye to eye with her, barking at the top of its voice. Some were tiny. She didn't like the way that the Pekingese was eyeing her ankles. And some of the dogs looked simply threatening looking, like the Pitbull mix that was sidling around the outside of the pack. Some, like the Labrador mixes in the middle, were going for sheer volume.

Katie felt her heart accelerate. This was a situation she'd never expected to be in. She'd been prepared for the threat of a violent human, but had been less prepared for the onslaught of a killer pack of hounds.

"Don't show your fear," she murmured to Leblanc.

"How do I not show my fear?" he hissed back in terrified tones as the lead dog rushed up to them, its barking and growling so loud that the sound waves battered Katie's face.

"Good dog," she tried in an appeasing voice, wishing that she'd brought some of the canine snacks that were for sale at the venue.

A troubling thought occurred to her that with a pack this big and aggressive, she and Leblanc might easily end up being the canine snacks themselves.

"Good, good dogs," she tried again. She reached out a hand and let the lead dog sniff her glove. The barking had died down now. Their tails were wagging - which was good - but they were still growling softly, and Katie guessed the jury was still out on whether the pack saw them as a threat or not.

"Nice doggies," she heard Leblanc say beside her. "Where's your owner, hey? Where's your owner? And if he's not here, are you going to let us go back to the car? We'd really like to wait there now."

And then, Katie's heart accelerated even faster as she heard another noise, one she recognized only too well.

It was the metallic click of a double-action shotgun being readied.

A moment later, a tall, lean man strolled around the house, with the gun in his hand.

"Who the hell are you?" he growled. "You'd better give me some straight answers. And no sudden moves. If you make 'em, I'll tell the pack to attack."

CHAPTER NINETEEN

"There's no need for that," Katie said, keeping as still as possible. She didn't know where to establish eye contact. With the lead dog, staring her down, or with its owner, gripping the shotgun as he glowered at her.

"We're law enforcement, here to ask a few questions in connection with the murders that have happened at the Sled Dog Festival. Are you Ed Knowles?"

She waited. The air felt very silent and filled with expectation.

And then, Knowles said, "I am, but how do I know that you're who you say you are? How can I trust you're telling the truth?"

"I can show you my police badge," Katie said. That would involve reaching into her parka to open the flap on her jacket. She wasn't sure who might be more triggered by this, Knowles or his pack.

"I'm going to have to look inside my jacket to show you," she said.

"Go ahead."

She stared at him. "Is there any possibility of - of asking your dogs to move just a step back? I don't want them jumping to the wrong conclusion."

He was silent for a moment.

Then he uttered one word, "Back!"

The pack immediately retreated a yard or so, giving Katie some much-appreciated breathing space to open her coat. However, this highlighted to her exactly how well trained the pack was. If he said, "Attack," what would happen?

She produced her FBI badge - not sure if it would help or inflame the situation - and held it out to him.

The Pekingese gave a warning yelp. One or two of the other dogs surged forward, teeth bared.

"Now, wait!" Knowles said angrily.

The Pekingese subsided, and the others followed suit.

"Thank you," Katie said, aware just how close she'd come to being terrorized by that little dog. She had no doubt at all as to which of these strong, healthy looking animals was the pack leader. Second in command only to Knowles, the Pekingese called the shots, it was clear.

Knowles studied the FBI badge for a long moment

"All right, I accept you're for real," he said at last. "Now, why are you here on my property? What questions do you have?"

Katie tried to keep her tone level and calm.

"There have been three murders that have taken place at the Sled Dog Festival, and we're looking into the motives."

"I heard about those. Rest their souls. But you suspect me?" Knowles asked.

"You were banned for life last year. So yes, it seems to me you have a motive."

Knowles stared at them for a moment.

Then he lowered his gun.

"Okay," he said. "Off, boys and girls. Go on, get away."

As if on cue, the pack of dogs turned their focus from Katie and Leblanc and headed off onto the grounds, capering and sniffing as if they hadn't been eyeballing them with dinner in mind a minute ago.

"You got the wrong guy," he said. "I don't have a motive."

Now, he didn't sound angry anymore. To her surprise, Katie realized he sounded a lot more reasonable.

"I think being banned for life is a pretty strong motive. Did Menzies do the legal work for that?"

Knowles shook his head. "He didn't. They used a non-local lawyer so as not to be accused of any bias. Besides, it's not a ban for life. It was originally going to be. But I appealed it, and the organizers, together with the international show holding body, assessed my appeal and they realized there had been fault on both sides. There was an earlier incident between me and the other man who said I was a cheat. Extenuating circumstances. I didn't take it further but in the previous incident he was the aggressor. So anyways, after weighing it up, they recently changed the lifetime ban to a three year suspension. I'm not sure if the original records have been updated yet, but I'm out of the race for three years, then I'm welcome back and can compete again."

"But - " Leblanc said, but Knowles powered on with his explanation.

"Furthermore, I don't need to compete to do well out of the race. A number of teams from all over the world buy and race my Alaskan Malamutes. I have champion bloodlines and they are top sled performers. A three-year ban now makes no difference to me. I have dogs in the race, running under my stud name. One of the teams is even tipped to win the long distance section this year. It's a USA team from Maine, and it's comprised of all my dogs."

"But where are your dogs?" Katie asked. "I didn't see any Alaskan Malamutes in the pack just now?"

"Those are my personal dogs," Knowles explained. "They're all rescues or adopted animals. I've got a big heart and can never say no to a dog in difficult circumstances. The breeding dogs are in the big barn. I have limited numbers, not more than four breeding females and two stud males at any one time. The pups are all booked up a year in advance, and as soon as they are twelve weeks old, they are shipped to their new owners, unless I get contracted to raise them for an extra month or two. My breeding dogs have luxury, insulated kennels, large exercise runs, and are all let out into the fenced area beyond, for exercise and play, all day. I was about to go and do that when you arrived. You're welcome to view them. My facilities are world class. I'm an example of an ethical breeder, who loves the dogs and produces sport-specific dogs, according to demand, and only what the sport needs."

Katie was feeling taken aback. She'd never expected that the circumstances of the ban would have changed, or that Knowles would have turned out to have such a big heart. With more perspective on the situation, it didn't seem like he was their killer.

Even so, just to make sure, she wanted to know if he had an alibi for any of the murders. She'd known psychopaths in the past who had been outspoken animal lovers, but lethal killers of humans. It was always better to check.

"Can you account for your whereabouts yesterday night at around eight p.m.?" she asked.

"Absolutely," Knowles said. "I was right here. I was with my friend Walter. He delivers dog food for me once a month. It's a long trip and I order a lot of dog food, so he and his son always stay over, and my wife and I cook for them. That's what I was doing last night at that time. I was right here, sitting around our kitchen table, eating a very good Irish stew, and drinking a couple of beers."

"Can Walter confirm that?"

"Sure. I'll give you his number. His truck has a tracker if you want to get the records from him. My wife is still in bed, as it ended up being a late night, but she can confirm it too."

"There's no need for that," Katie said. "Don't wake her. If you can give me Walter's number, it'll be fine. And thank you for your time."

"Sorry for being suspicious at the start," Knowles explained. "I have had issues in the past, where people have snuck in and tried to steal my dogs. I was worried that you were thieves and I'd caught you in the act."

"It's been good meeting you," Katie said, as they exchanged details. She was pleasantly surprised by the fact that under his threatening exterior, Knowles seemed to be a genuinely good guy, if a little rough around the edges, as many here were.

He gave her the details, and they said goodbye.

The only problem with having Knowles cleared was that they had no other suspects now. This had been the only disgruntled competitor that their search had uncovered. This drive into the cold wilderness had ended up being for nothing. Now, it was eight a.m. and the day was starting. The festival would be open and the races under way.

And Katie had no doubt that, already, their killer would be on the prowl.

They climbed into the car, in thoughtful silence.

"Okay, so it wasn't a competitor then. But there might be other people who want the race abolished," Katie said.

"Like who?" Leblanc asked.

"I don't know. But I'm remembering now, when we spoke to Mr. Pope, how adamant he was that the race never gets canceled. The way he was talking, I'm now wondering if anyone complained about it in the past."

"So Pope's our next stop?" Leblanc sounded enthused at this idea.

"Perhaps this isn't his first rodeo," Katie elaborated. "Perhaps he has had serious complaints. Now, someone's trying to force his hand, and it might well be that he knows who that someone is."

CHAPTER TWENTY

Sitting in front of him an hour later, Katie thought that Mr. Pope, the festival organizer, looked as if he'd aged a few years since yesterday. Clearly, the pressure was weighing on him. His dark hair was spiky and in disarray. His face was pale under the tan. His eyes were reddened and the dark rings underneath told her that he'd slept badly, if at all.

Katie felt sorry for a moment that she and Leblanc were only going to make things worse.

"I have two requests," she said.

Mr. Pope looked at her dubiously.

"What are those?" he asked in a voice that told her he was at the end of his patience.

"Firstly, please. Shut things down here. At any rate, postpone the start of the actual festival till tomorrow? Just until we've caught this killer. It's an issue of safety. And it's for the longevity of the festival. If you value this event, if you want to hold it in the future, please call it off. One more death, will mean the death-knell for it."

"I've already seen a few guests canceling," Pope admitted. Feeling as if she might have a chance, Katie pressed her point.

"At least, postpone the major celebration. The party after the race, the big music performance, the outdoor activities. Those are going to draw crowds, and at this stage, every person here is in danger."

Pope shook his head.

"Agent Winter, some people have left. But not many. People understand - from what I've heard them say - that this killer must be targeting people for a reason. Not just random festival goers. For example, tragic as it is, the last victim was the lawyer, Ivan Menzies. Ivan has nothing to do with the festival. I know him personally because he assists our family with legal matters. But he's never been involved in the organization of the event, and the signs are that he was taken from his home, or so the police tell me."

94

He looked at her with shrewd, if exhausted, eyes. "Based on this last tragedy, how exactly is staying home going to help?"

Katie pressed her lips together. Next to her, she heard Leblanc sigh uneasily. She had to admit that Pope had a point.

"Where were you when this murder happened?" she asked, wondering briefly if Pope might have a darker reason for wanting the festival to continue. She knew that his ego and his investment were all rooted in it, but it suddenly occurred to her that if he was the killer, a carefully hidden psychopath in a businessman's guise, it wouldn't suit his purposes to have it shut down.

"Last night? I was at a dignitaries' dinner from about six, with my brother. It was at the main hotel in town. I got the call at about eight-thirty and I left the dinner. My brother and I reopened the organizer's office, as I was being inundated with calls. Jason stayed to help for an hour or so before he headed home."

Katie felt satisfied this had cleared him and that he could not have been in the right place at the right time to commit the murders himself.

"We've got police from neighboring towns coming in to boost the numbers of law enforcement on site. Security is paramount. But since the last victim was taken from his home," Pope said again, meaningfully, "catching the killer is obviously more important than shutting the festival down. So how can I help? Anything, and I mean anything I can do, I will do."

Leblanc cleared his throat and Katie knew he was going ahead with the next question, the crucial one, that they had discussed earlier in the car.

"As the organizer, you would know better than the police if there is anyone who's opposed to this festival, correct?"

"That's a very difficult question because it benefits the whole town. Ever since Jason bought the land a few years ago, which has helped me immensely as it's the most sheltered area in Soaring Crow, my aim has been to grow this festival, to make it a high point on the calendar, to improve it and make it the biggest event that there is in the dog racing world. And the town has been fully behind me on this."

"Everyone?" Katie asked. Now she had the meaningful tone in her voice.

Pope sighed. "Almost everyone. There are always the negative ones, the naysayers, the people who manufacture problems. But those are minor."

"A minor problem to you might be a major issue to a psychopath who sees the world differently," Katie said. "To that person, it will be a reason to kill. So right now, those minor niggles are important."

Leblanc took a deep breath. "Mr. Pope, I can see you are a positive person. You do not like to dwell on the negative, nor think about it. But for now, you need to. Because in those negative comments, the killer may be hiding."

Pope nodded reluctantly. "True. True, I get you. And you're right. I abhor negativity. Okay then. Let me think."

As if he needed to gather his fragmented thoughts, he rested his forehead in his hands for a few moments. Katie waited, wondering if he was going to come up with a suspect. She hoped so. Someone must have their own reason for shutting down this festival.

"There was that animal rights activist," he said thoughtfully. "What was her name?"

"Julia Marr?" Katie said, and Pope made a face.

"I can see you're ahead of me on this. Let me think again."

For another few moments there was silence in the busy office. And then, a voice spoke from behind Pope. It was the voice of his young assistant, who was hard at work at the other desk.

"Remember that meeting you had the other day? That man threatened he was going to go to the media."

"Yes, but he was completely delusional," Pope said amiably. "A man like that, how can you take him seriously?"

"He's sounding as if he might need to be taken seriously. Someone like this could be exactly the person we need," Katie said. "Who is he?"

She was all the more intrigued now because it was clear this person had not yet approached the media. So the Soaring Crow Community News, where they'd asked questions yesterday, wouldn't have known about him.

"He's a man called Chris Czerny," Pope admitted.

"And who is he? His role in this town?" Leblanc asked.

"He's an environmentalist. He teaches online, and holds classes on Monday and Tuesday at a college in Fork River, which is a town about two hundred miles to the south of here. He commutes, and sleeps over at the college on those days, but the rest of the time, he's here. He's said many times that he wants to turn the world into a sustainable society, a society where people don't live in a way that destroys the environment."

"And what's his gripe with the festival?"

"He says that the numbers of dogs and the number of people are going to bring development to the town that will destroy its character, and he's also worried about plants, or some such issue. Which is nonsense of course, as the majority of visitors are only here for a short while, three or four weeks at most, and we are able to temporarily accommodate them. And it's in winter. Plants don't grow in winter, right?"

"How long has he been here?" Katie's heart was beating faster now. This was the type of lead she had been hoping for.

"Couple of years, I think. He moved north when they began mining in his old town, and from what he told me, he was looking for a more peaceful environment."

Katie could see that Pope was a very busy man, who had focused only on the positives of the festival, and because of this, he'd taken little notice of someone he regarded as a minor troublemaker. But she felt very glad they now knew about Chris Czerny.

"He sounds like someone we need to speak to," Katie said. That was a direct motive for wanting to damage the festival. There was a very clear link between what Czerny had complained about, and the effect the killings were having.

"Personality wise, what is he like?"

"He's a difficult one. He can be very charming, very logical and persuasive, and then change in a flash and become threatening and unreasonable and aggressive," Pope admitted.

Katie felt a flare of excitement. These personality traits were most definitely pointing the way to a potentially psychopathic streak.

"We'll go and question him right away," she said, standing up. "Thank you for the lead - and for now, please, keep on being careful."

CHAPTER TWENTY ONE

Within a few minutes, after some quick research on the way out the door, Katie had an address for the environmentalist Chris Czerny. He lived a few miles out of town, on a small, off the grid farm that, according to the map, was bordered by forest on three sides. She knew there was no time to waste in going there.

He had a strong motive, as a passionate supporter of the environment who'd already had to relocate because of mining starting up in his previous town. And furthermore, he showed the personality traits of a possible psychopath. That ability to change in a flash from charming to irrational was raising red flags for her, and she saw Leblanc was also looking thoughtful as they rushed to the car.

Katie got in and drove out of town, heading down a rutted dirt road, clogged with snow and patterned with weaving tire tracks.

"He could be a psychopath, based on the behavior?" Leblanc said.

"He's a very likely candidate."

"So are you going to be able to use a technique to prove that, or prod him in any way to reveal who he is?"

"I don't know," Katie said. "It will depend on the circumstances. Ultimately, I think the alibi will be a more important tool here. It'll be down to hard facts, and making sure he doesn't duck and dive when we ask him to give his whereabouts."

She was feeling as if this upcoming confrontation was going to be all important, and she had no idea what to expect. Would Mr. Reasonable be waiting for them when they climbed out of the car, or would it be Mr. Deranged that they had to deal with?

"He lives in the middle of nowhere," Leblanc said, as the car jolted over yet another hidden rock.

"Maybe that's deliberate. And maybe that's what he wants, to be away from people and to keep people away from him. And he is using this as a way to achieve his aims."

Katie kept her misgivings about this upcoming interview to herself, and said nothing more until they had turned off the road and bumped along a short distance through the trees. They pulled up after driving through an open gateway, in front of a beautiful log cabin. It was neat and pristine, flanked by handsome pine trees. Solar panels on the south-facing roof and insulated rainwater tanks near the cabin emphasized to her that this man lived off the grid and utilized nature's resources.

An electric car was parked under a neat carport, well insulated with a layer of straw bales.

"Well, it looks idyllic," she said doubtfully.

That didn't mean that a cold-blooded murderer did not occupy this well-tended property, she reminded herself.

She knew from her own experience that there was no scientific way of proving that a person was a psychopath. There were no physical tests, no DNA tests, nothing that could be used to prove a person had the traits she'd calculated for the killer.

At the same time, she had been working in an investigative unit for a long time now and she'd had her fair share of gut feelings over the years. And her gut was telling her that this behavior meant something.

They climbed out of the car into a cold, biting wind. The clouds were even lower now. There was a heaviness in the air, a sense of threat.

She walked along the well-swept path to the front door, and knocked. Leblanc stood by her side and they waited, expectantly, as footsteps approached.

The door was pulled open and Katie found herself looking at a slim, fit looking man with a thatch of straw-like hair. He gave her a friendly smile. It was an innocent looking smile, and Katie thought how easy he would be to trust. Until you noticed his eyes. His eyes were cold as they looked at her face, and then down at her badge.

"This is very unusual. Two plainclothes detectives on my doorstep?" Czerny sounded inquiring. "Can I help you?"

"Mr. Czerny? We need to ask you some questions," Katie said.

"That's me. And such a discussion would probably be better done inside. This wind is particularly strong today. A pity with so many visitors in town," Czerny said, with a shrug that conveyed a marked lack of sympathy. Katie raised internal eyebrows at this. It was obvious that Czerny was indeed opposed to the perceived intrusion.

Now to find out how far he'd taken this opinion.

They stepped into a room that was warm, with the fireplace piled with logs. A fire was already crackling away and Katie could feel the heat on her face. There was a sofa, comfortable looking chairs, and a large laptop with a green screen background positioned against one wall.

"I have a class in twenty minutes," Czerny said, glancing at the laptop. "Can we be brief?"

Katie took a seat. "That depends, Mr. Czerny. Let me explain why we're here."

"Go ahead?" He raised an eyebrow, but without any warmth.

"We're here because we understand you are opposed to the festival. And that you've been outspoken in telling the organizer it should be shut down."

"The festival where the murders have occurred? Don't you also think that bringing such high numbers of visitors to this small town is causing a surge in crime?" he countered.

Katie thought they were still getting the charming side of him - just.

"You have a motive for committing these murders," she stated.

"No. I'm a peaceful man," Czerny said, but there was a sudden tension in his shoulders. "I have the right to express my views, and I have done so. I have not threatened anyone - I would never threaten anyone," he stated, looking straight at her.

"Yesterday evening, where were you?"

He looked down.

"Where were you?" Leblanc echoed sternly.

Czerny sighed. "I was at the festival."

Katie's eyes widened. He was there, and had admitted to it?

"And can you account for your time there? Were you with anyone? Why were you there if you were so opposed to it?" she pressured him.

Czerny shrugged. "It would be pointless opposing something without doing enough research on it. And I was there on my own. I didn't travel with anyone. I live alone."

"What about the previous day? Can you account for your time then?"

The air seemed filled with tension and she thought that, without a doubt, Czerny was going to snap and they would see the side that Pope had warned them about.

And then, he shook his head briefly. To Katie's surprise, he gave her a rueful smile that did warm his eyes this time.

"I feel that the entire principle of the festival is based on unfairness. Those were ancient lands originally traversed by First Nation people, and since they were claimed, and sold, and resold piecemeal, it's all been done in a spirit of unfairness which I have followed in great detail. But over and above the ethical reasons, let's talk about ecology. There are a few threatened species growing in the area that are highly environmentally sensitive. If the festival spreads further, if its footprint increases, it's going to be destructive."

"Your time yesterday and the day before?" Katie reminded him, getting back to the point and deciding not to fall for his charm.

"I was speaking to some of the influencers in town. The leading business people, the town's kingpins. I want to organize a meeting to set some limitations. I had to do it without Pope knowing. He presses all my wrong buttons. If there's one person who can get me to lose my temper it's him. His brother is much more diplomatic than he is, but Pope's the one I have to deal with. So that's what I was doing there. And the previous day, I taught an extra day and evening class at the university. I only got back yesterday morning. The class ended at eight p.m. and when I teach that late, I sleep over."

"Do you have proof of that?"

"Sure. I can show you my booking, I can show you my parking pass, and I can show you the restaurant check."

He opened his wallet, and within a minute, had presented Katie with the proof.

"I'm not a murderous man. I'm a deeply concerned man. I don't want the town to suffer as a result of this festival. I personally think that someone is doing this to protect the land. In a way, it's inevitable. I am very in tune with nature. Land issues go so deep here."

"You think so?" Katie asked.

"I do. And I'm surprised you're not at the festival now, and that you took the time to travel all the way out here."

"Why's that?"

He checked his watch. "Because the winning long distance team is coming in, in about half an hour, I should think. And with all the crowds and excitement, aren't you worried it's a risky time? Surely you have a better chance of catching the killer there, on site?"

"Of course we are worried," Katie said. "And yes, we're heading back now."

This news had shaken her.

She hadn't known that the lead team was coming in so soon. Events felt as if they were accelerating all the way out of control. As soon as that team crossed the finish line, the festival would get under way.

And then she thought Czerny was right. The killer might well be looking to use this time to take another victim. All bets would be off, and all safety would be at risk.

They needed to get back there, and fast.

CHAPTER TWENTY TWO

Half an hour later, as Katie sped up to the festival grounds, she saw immediately that the atmosphere had changed. The festival grounds were seething with visitors. More crowds were thronging in. The parking lot was full, bursting at the seams with cars, and Katie had to drive all the way to the end of the row, bumping along the packed snow, gritting her teeth as she thought about the risk.

"I can see why Pope didn't want to cancel, though," she acknowledged, looking at all the out-of-province and foreign plates that were among the vehicles. Some of them had probably driven for a couple of days to get here, and for them to turn back would have been a logistical nightmare. Furthermore, Katie guessed they were already looking at a scenario in which some guests had chosen to change their plans. Without the murders it would probably have been even busier.

Perhaps, with all the dangers inherent in dog racing out in the cold wilderness, the attendees had a higher appetite for risk.

But now, for certain, they were going to have a security challenge on their hands. Every person at the event was potentially in danger until the killer was caught.

"Where in these crowds is he hiding?" Leblanc muttered. It was a given, Katie thought, that he was here somewhere.

As she climbed out, she saw two uniformed RCMP officers patrolling the parking area, looking closely at all the arrivals. One of the officers walked purposefully over to a man who was heading into the festival on his own.

"Excuse me, sir. Do you have any weapons on you? Any knives, guns?" he asked, quickly running a handheld scanner over his clothing.

"I'm all clear, of course," the man said, sounding surprised and not too pleased about being stopped.

"Go ahead, please, sir. It's a precautionary check. Keeping things safe for everyone."

They waved him along and he headed for the entrance kiosk where tickets were being purchased and a line was already forming.

So they were trying, Katie thought. Most definitely, precautions were in place. Likely looking prospects were being identified and checked.

The problem was that the festival ground was such a big, fluid place. It wasn't securely fenced, but only cordoned off near the parking, to allow for the ticket sales. And the killer, if he'd been smart, could easily have concealed a weapon somewhere.

Additionally, Katie was sure that the sled drivers all had legitimate weapons on their person. She didn't see anyone setting off on a thousand mile sled ride involving teams of dogs, without carrying several sharp knives to be used in an emergency.

She wished she could figure out more accurately what this killer really wanted and why he was doing what he did. What was his agenda, over and above to kill? How was he choosing his victims - because he clearly was, but there was still no pattern that they could see that could lead back to him. It was so frustrating.

Or was there one, that she was sensing, but not yet managing to join all the dots?

Sighing to herself, watching her breath puff out in white, misty clouds against the ominously gray sky, Katie felt there was something she was missing. There had been something that had gotten her mind working earlier. It had been a seed planted in her thoughts, during the conversation with the environmentalist. She wished she had more time to explore it, to sit alone, quietly, reviewing the case notes and trying to strengthen the tenuous connection, the mental leap she'd made, based on something Czerny had said.

If only.

But there was no time now, because the risk was too immediate, and they needed to get feet on the ground, and eyes on the lookout.

Already, Katie could hear the boom of the loudspeakers, followed by cheers, and the now familiar sound of the warning whistles. The long distance teams were approaching. After days spent in the icy wilderness, and an arduous race, the excitement of the finish was drawing the crowds, and the first teams would pass the line soon.

Without a doubt, this was a time of highest risk. She felt, with a chill, that the killer might be building to a crescendo, intending to make a statement by leaving a victim right here. To show off, to prove a point that only he understood and Katie hadn't yet caught up with.

She felt cold with apprehension.

She walked to the entrance kiosk first, together with Leblanc. There were three RCMP officers there, all looking worried and businesslike.

"Good morning," the closest one greeted them. "So far so good, things seem quiet. But it's going to get even busier than it is now, as more people arrive."

"We'll be heading to the finish line," Katie said. "Keeping an eye on things there, while the first few teams cross the line."

"If you need any backup, we're right here," the officer assured her. "Just shout, and we'll get there as fast as we can."

"And likewise," Katie said, before heading through the kiosk and down towards the gathered crowds.

As she left, she heard arriving guests asking, "Morning. Can you confirm if it's safe today? We heard there were a couple of crimes here last night, but accounts are very confused. Someone said it was a fight between locals, and someone else said that it was one of the racers who didn't win. Will we be okay as long as we leave before dark?"

Katie could hear, from listening, that the grapevine had been working overtime.

Everyone had a different view of why these killings had occurred. She thought from this conversation that the people who hadn't canceled perceived it as a fight between locals, rather than a danger to anyone who was present.

Maybe the town's grapevine had more inherent insight into the reasons than she herself did, she wondered. But she knew the situation could change in a flash if the killer struck again. There was no doubt that the success and future longevity of this festival was on a knife edge.

"We have a strong police presence here, and you can shout for help if you notice anything worrying," the officer said, and Katie could hear he was trying his best to sound reassuring, without actually giving false information. "So far, it's all been quiet and folks are enjoying themselves, but we are advising everyone to take care."

Katie walked on. The festival ground was very sheltered, thanks to the thick banks of forest, she noticed again. It was most definitely an area cradled and protected from the ferocity of the weather beyond.

The sounds of a live band playing could be heard from a distance. Families were strolling around the stalls, with kids bundled up in colorful packages of parkas, scarves, and boots. She smelled the sizzle of cooking food, the aroma of coffee. There were even magicians and crowd entertainers at work. She saw clowns doing impromptu comedy acts, a man in a polar bear suit and another in a reindeer outfit, and a juggler sending colored balls soaring high into the air. This truly was a festival where no detail had gone ignored, and Katie had to admire the amount of work and passion that had gone into it.

"Where do we go?" Leblanc asked, looking around him.

"We get a good vantage point, close to the finish line," she said. "And we keep an eye out."

"For what? Anything in particular you have been able to figure out, any profile for this guy?"

She shook her head. "I don't know. It's so frustrating. There's something that is bothering me, something I think I should be considering, but I'm not sure what it is. So for now, I don't know. I figure we just have to do our best to spot anyone acting suspiciously."

She knew that the winning team was hurtling toward the finish, and could come in at any moment. Her heart was racing as she made her way through the crowd.

Ahead, on the path that led to the finish line, she saw a cluster of people standing, watching, exclaiming, and pointing at the rows of dogs in the distance. The teams were in sight and excitement was peaking.

Now she could sense the growing anticipation of the crowd, as they cheered and whistled, shouting for their favorites. Ahead, stacks of straw bales with sponsors' banners affixed lined the track. Brightly colored flags flapped and twisted in the breeze. On the other side of the finish were several large marquees, as well as a roped off rest area for the dogs, with bright signage from the dog food sponsors.

"It's going to be a neck and neck finish," one of the women said excitedly as they passed, and Katie couldn't help a shiver of apprehension at the thought that all the kills had been done by slashing open the victims' necks. "Did you see Aaron West winning the sprint race just now? That was close, but this looks to be even closer. Amazing, for a long-distance race to be so closely fought at the finish line."

Yet again, Katie felt that her mind was reaching for a connection, for something important, but she could not grasp it.

Shaking her head, Katie wondered whether it was a real theory at all, or whether she was just imagining things now, desperate to make some kind of logical connection when there was none.

"Over here," she said, spotting a place right near the finish line. "We have a good view here. And we can see the crowds.

The cheers and shouts were building. Some watchers were holding up their phones, ready to capture the big moment, and others were waving banners with the various team colors.

"It's the Malamutes!" someone shouted triumphantly. "Jett and the Malamutes are going to do it!"

She could see it now. A team of Alaskan Malamutes was racing toward them. The driver, a man dressed in red, was hunkered down over the sled, intent on the finish line as he held off the second place winner, who was a man wearing green, with a team of huskies.

"Come on, Jett," someone shouted, as the jubilant crowd started chanting. "Come on, you can do it. You're almost there. You've got it!"

"Go, Graham and the Huskies!" someone else yelled.

The dogs were racing at full tilt, and the crowd was applauding and whistling clear and loud in the still, cold air. Katie could see the growing speed of the dogs at the front of the sled, their eager faces as they raced along, clearly fit and thriving despite the long distance and cold conditions.

"It's a race, it's a race, it's a race," a little boy chanted, laughing, and hopping from foot to foot.

Katie's heart was pounding as she watched the sleds approaching.

Where was he?

She tried to think, to calm herself, to reason through the situation rationally. She knew she had to be clear-headed, to be ready for anything that was about to happen.

There were hundreds of people here. He could be anywhere. He could be watching, in the crowd. He could be near the finish line, waiting for a chance to strike. Soon, she feared it was going to be over, one way or another. But she had to stop this. If her own vigilance could make the difference between life and death, then she wasn't going to do as much as blink until the killer was caught.

"Here come the teams from British Columbia," another woman said. "They're looking strong! I'm betting on them to take first."

"No, no, Jett's got it. He's got this one in the bag!" someone else shouted.

"Jett, you did it!" someone shouted, as the lead dogs crossed the finish line. The crowd erupted in a roar of excitement.

"Yes! Jett, you did it! You won it!" a woman was shrieking, waving her red banner.

"Let's go and congratulate him," someone else said.

In the festive atmosphere, people were moving around, swarming in, so that officials had to ask the crowds to stand back as the dogs were unharnessed.

So far, everything had gone smoothly, Katie thought. So far, it looked as if they had been wrong that the killer would want to use the finish of the race as his own personal grand finale. Perhaps he would wait until night to kill again – but since the festival would continue until night fell, it meant they would have to keep alert and on the watch for a good few more hours.

She watched as the driver of the winning team leapt from the sled and made his way to the edge of the crowd, where he was being mobbed by fellow racers and dog handlers.

The dogs were being praised and checked by Jett's team, offered water and treats, before being led over for the vet inspection.

Katie saw the red-coated winner raising his arms in victory, laughing. Two of his team members, also in red, were by his side. And a third was approaching.

Only this one, this man coming toward Jett - he didn't look like a team member. He wasn't in red. He wasn't even approaching Jett from the front, but was sneaking in from the side.

There was a strange intent to his body language that got Katie's attention and she stepped forward, her stomach clenching in apprehension.

"Leblanc, look." She grabbed his arm, drawing in a horrified breath as she saw the man was holding something behind his back. Cupped in his gloved hand, Katie saw the gleam of shiny steel.

The killer? Was she watching the killer himself?

And then, the man moved suddenly forward, bringing his hand up.

"No! Stop!"

Yelling at the top of her voice, Katie raced toward them.

CHAPTER TWENTY THREE

The man in the coat was ready. He'd waited for so long, been so patient. This was the culmination of his plans, the result of careful, meticulous, and yet bloody work.

He had identified each of the targets he needed. All of them were of great significance in this journey of death. Each one represented a triumph, a win, the ascendancy of right over wrong.

Each one represented his own personal payback. The man in the coat had observed them, learned everything he could, and then had done what he needed to do.

He'd been ready months ago, had been waiting and watching, but the time was not right.

He'd been so patient, knowing that the waiting was essential and that the kills needed to be grouped together - fast and deadly - if he was going to be able to complete his mission.

He had been willing to wait, to see it through, to make sure that every step of his plan came to fruition.

Now, it was finally here. Today was the day of the race. It was his final performance, the last act. It was about vindication. The last of the targets was going to meet his fate today.

Smiling at the thought, he watched the scene around him. The colorful arch of the finish line, the stacks of hay bales providing a winner's enclosure, the grounds dotted with stalls and entertainment. From this vantage point, he could see everything.

The crowds were cheering. People were milling around, laughing and joking, eating and drinking, enjoying the festival.

They'd all know about his final triumph. But perhaps nobody except him would understand the reasons. And that was fine. The man in the coat was happy for those reasons to stay personal. They were his, and his alone. Only he knew the deep significance of doing what he did.

And only he had the power, thanks to the blade that was concealed deep in his pocket.

He'd hidden it away last night, guessing that in the morning, on this big day, there might well be searches at the gates. And there had been. Sure enough, he'd been searched, by a very apologetic RCMP officer.

It had made him very pleased to think that he was a step ahead here, that he hadn't been caught out by this security precaution. Perhaps the police were thinking the same thing. Perhaps they were feeling pleased by their hard work, congratulating themselves on their vigilance in checking bags and searching bodies and other things.

But they would never have found the blade. He had been careful to hide it well. Overnight, it had been buried deep in one of the bales of straw that had been placed out on the snow for people to use as seats, and this morning he had sat down, reached into the bale, and grasped its solid handle. Now, with it in his grasp but hidden from view, he stood again.

"Excuse me," he said, smiling in apology as he jostled a woman who was slurping from her coffee mug.

"Oh, sorry," she said, stepping aside with a smile.

This small interaction confirmed to the man in the coat that he was being seen as normal. Nobody was paying him any attention. That was a good sign. He didn't want anyone to see what he was about to do, to look at him and guess what his plan was, to wonder why he was here at this place, at this very moment.

Nobody suspected him for who he was. And that meant he was going to get away with this. He was going to be able to take the biggest prize of all, the one he had been building up to.

Saving the best for last. He gave a cold grin at the thought.

And then, he would disappear, melting back into society, unknown and undiscovered. It gave him a fierce joy to know that he would have outwitted the police, the special detectives, most probably even the FBI representative that he had seen on the news that was now involved. None of them were as smart as he was, and all of them were lagging far behind, soon to be outpaced forever, like the losers in a race.

They would have the humiliation of a cold case, never solved, never discovered. A blot on their record, and a permanent scar in the success of the festival. Most probably after what he planned to do, it would be stopped.

And he would have the satisfaction of knowing he'd done it, that he had taken his own personal revenge in the most final way. It gave him a bitter amusement to think of how they would feel, the people who thought they were so smart, so clever, so good at their jobs. That they hadn't been able to find him.

Now, he was close. The last target was here. And at last, he could take that final step. He could make his final strike. He felt the urge to do it again, as his mind surged into action, figuring out the final details, who would be where. It felt more like a game of chess than a race. Strategy, planning, and then quick violence. This time – to continue the chess theme – the king would be taken and the game would be won.

The man in the coat wanted to cry out in triumph. He wanted to scream around the block, to let everyone know that he had achieved what he set out to do. But he couldn't do that, of course. What he had done, and what he knew, must never be shared.

The plan must never be discovered. The killings must be kept secret, must be buried, hidden away, and never spoken about. So he had to keep the tumult of his emotions to himself.

In any case, he could not start celebrating until the final job was done. Anticipation was a beautiful thing, but he couldn't get carried away before the time. If he was going to achieve his aims, he had to be careful. He had to be stealthy. He had to be sneaky.

And he had to make sure that no one stopped him.

In the front of the sled, the winning driver was accepting congratulations, laughing, clapping his teammates on the back, guzzling champagne from a bottle.

He saw a young man with a victorious smile on his face, waving at the crowd. He was giving a thumbs up to his adoring fans, who were doting on him, hailing him as a hero.

He was the winner, the winner of the race.

The man in the coat knew he had chosen his moment well. A crowd had gathered around the driver of the winning team, and now the organizers were on their way to congratulate him. He was accepting claps on the back, handshakes, and hugs.

"Congratulations on the win."

"You did it, Jett! Great job! Way to go!"

"Brilliant tactics! Your team was so strong, the whole way through!"

The racer seemed to be basking in the attention. He smiled and laughed, shaking his head.

"No, no, it was all of us, a team's not just one person. We all did it together. This is an honor, an honor to be part of this. It's a privilege to win this."

"This is the best teamwork I've ever seen," added another team member. "And your dogs are in superb condition."

"I'll drink to that," said the driver, raising his bottle of champagne. "To the best dogs ever, bred by a champion!"

"We need to move through for a photo op just now. As soon as the first three teams are ready, we're going to have podium pics with the organizer and the VIPs," one of the assistants said.

Everyone was distracted, too busy to notice what was happening. But he was going to ensure they did notice, very soon. They would be in no doubt at all as to what was happening here.

He had a job to do, a responsibility to acknowledge, a duty to fulfill. He had a right, and he was going to use it.

This was an ending, he thought, a repayment for all the horrendous crimes that had been perpetrated on him. Nobody would understand that, of course. Nobody would ever know the truth.

The man in the coat glanced around him, making sure that nobody was watching.

Then he moved swiftly forward, his hand gripping the knife handle.

CHAPTER TWENTY FOUR

"No!" Screaming at the top of her voice, Katie rushed forward, barging through the crowds. She was yelling, pushing, desperate to cause a distraction, to derail the catastrophe that was about to explode in their faces.

He was there. The killer. Moving up, raising his arm, ready to stab, in full view of the crowds. And he was going to do it.

"Stop! Clear out of the way!" Katie screamed.

She saw the man raise his hand, saw the flash of metal as the blade was pulled out of the pocket. She was ten feet away, and she was going to be too late. The blade was going to hit its mark, and the man in the sled who was busy speaking to one of his team, was going to die.

"No, I won't let you!" she shouted, roaring out the words at the top of her voice, so that other people would hear what she was saying, so that the killer might hear, and could be distracted by the sound.

And it worked.

The man with the knife hesitated for just a moment. He glanced around. And that was enough. It gave her the moment she needed.

Katie launched herself at him.

He recoiled, his eyes wide and his mouth open in shock as he saw her coming at him. Clumsily thrown off guard, he scrambled backward, his feet slipping on the ice.

She lunged forward, faster than she had ever moved before. She threw herself against him, crashing right into him, knocking him off balance.

He dropped the knife. It clattered against the ground, and she kicked it, sending it spinning away out of his reach.

Swearing, he dove for his weapon, and Katie tackled him, using all her weight to try and get him down.

The man was a big guy. He was around six-feet-two and strongly built. And he was angry, ready to retaliate, his fists bunched. But he didn't move quickly enough. Katie still got to him first. She knocked him over with the force of her tackle.

He crashed into the pile of hay bales at the finish line, sending them tumbling to the side.

As they fell in a tangle of arms and legs, he tried to grab at her, his hands strong, but she jerked away, wrenching herself out of his grasp.

The man flailed wildly at her. He struck out, a fist catching her on the side of the face. He was brutally strong. The blow snapped her head back and she staggered, fighting for her balance. And she found it.

Drawing on the relentless sequences of combat training that she'd done at the FBI academy, instinct took over. She lashed out with her foot, and watched it connect squarely with his knee.

He stumbled backward, tripped, and fell down, sprawling among the scattered bales. And this time, Katie was on him. She was fast enough. She got a knee in his back, and one arm behind him.

And then, Leblanc was there, too, by her side, wrenching the man's other arm behind him and fastening the handcuffs. With a thunder of boots, two more RCMP officers rushed up.

"Back, please. Get back. Clear the scene, people. Give us some space," one of the officers said calmly, as she and Leblanc dragged the knifeman to his feet.

Katie scrambled up, breathing hard, hanging onto him tightly, feeling stunned that she'd managed to get to this would-be killer in time.

The fight had played out so fast that most of the others were still in shock, wondering what was going on. She saw the crowds, and the other racers, watching in surprise and confusion. Everyone was asking everyone else what had just happened. They looked stunned and shaken. Jett was looking utterly shocked. Quickly, needing some confirmation, Katie turned to him.

"Do you know this man?" she asked him, swinging him around so that the race winner could take a look at the knifeman's face. "He was about to attack you. Do you recognize him?"

Jett blinked, looking astounded.

"Yeah, yeah. I recognize him. He's Matt Taylor. We've raced against each other before now. I didn't even know he was here!"

His face darkened. He closed his mouth. It was one of the other team members who then spoke.

"He's always been a big rival. And hasn't always played by the rules. We've had problems with him in the past, but not at this level. It looks like he's just escalated them."

"Thank you," Katie said. So there was a connection here. That was what she needed to know, for now.

Matt Taylor was swearing, spluttering, and struggling as the RCMP officers took over, grabbing him by his shoulders and shunting him away from the crowds, who were still abuzz with consternation.

"What's happening?" someone called, sounding scared.

"We've identified a criminal and he's been arrested, ma'am," the RCMP officer reassured her. "He'll cause no further danger and we're taking him into custody immediately."

Katie decided the best thing they could do was to remove Matt Taylor from the area as fast as possible. He was causing a commotion, and she didn't want him to end up ruining the race just by his mere presence there, even though he'd been prevented from achieving his aims.

No longer could this struggling, violent man be the center of attention here, detracting from the joy and success of what was now going to be a safe occasion. Because at last, they had caught the killer.

"Let's take him straight to the police department," she told the officers. "We can process him there, and then question him."

"Good call," the nearest officer agreed, staring at Taylor with angry dislike. "What the hell was that about, anyway?"

"We're going to find out," Katie threatened. "About everything."

Katie and Leblanc walked ahead, leading the way out of the festival grounds, heading for the car.

Leblanc got the knifeman in the back and sat with him. The RCMP officer got in on the other side, and Katie climbed in the driver's seat.

As she headed out of the crowded parking lot, on the route to the RCMP offices, she couldn't help feeling a massive sense of relief that this was finally over. At the last possible moment she'd been able to intervene and catch this man. She didn't want to think what would have happened if he had not hesitated, had not heard her.

They had the man. It had been so close, so dangerous. With a moment to spare, she had saved Jett from serious injury and possible death. She had prevented the attack that would have traumatized onlookers and marred the festival, forming part of its record forever.

She glanced in the rearview mirror.

Looking back at her, the bearded Taylor glared at her with hatred in his dark eyes.

Katie accelerated down the road. Hate me all you like, she thought. But you're not going to get out of prison for a long, long time to come. With any luck, an angry look is the most damage you'll be able to do to anyone from here on out.

She stopped outside the police department, and they all got out and hustled Taylor inside.

"We're bringing in a suspect who attempted to murder the race winner at the finish line," Katie said to the officer in attendance. "We need to process his arrest, and then take him straight in for interrogation."

She hoped that having been caught red-handed, Taylor would confess to the other crimes. But there was no guarantee of that. He could try to duck and dive; he could decide that he was going to deny everything.

While the RCMP officers were processing their criminal, Katie headed straight to the interview room. Setting up what she needed and making sure the recording equipment was working, Katie knew she'd need to bring all her skills to this interrogation.

She wanted this wrapped up, and fast.

Footsteps and voices signaled to her that Taylor was being transferred, and a moment later, Leblanc and an RCMP officer brought him in, still handcuffed, and still angry.

They sat him down on the far side of the desk, and the RCMP officer fastened his cuffs to the chair, which was bolted to the floor, so that there was no danger of this big, heavy man causing any trouble.

For the first time, Katie took a good look at the killer - or rather, the suspected killer, she confirmed, because proof of the other crimes was still needed.

He was a thickset, heavy man with a broad face, dark eyes, and a bulky jaw that was covered in a dark, dense beard. Bushy eyebrows and a low brow seemed to exaggerate the frown on his face.

"Mr. Taylor. You're arrested for attempted murder, but we have other charges to bring against you also," Katie said, after she'd set the recorder up and read him his rights.

He stared at her sullenly.

"You know Jett Anders, the race winner?" she asked.

For a while she thought he wasn't going to answer. He glowered at her angrily. She picked up waves of malice emanating from him.

Katie guessed that this was going to be a long struggle. They were in for a tug of war to get to the truth. Taylor wasn't going to make this easy.

"I want a lawyer," he said. "I'm not talking until I get my lawyer. I know my rights, and I am going to demand them. You can't intimidate me."

"Okay," Katie said, accepting there was going to be an inevitable wait. "I'll get the phone and you can call your lawyer."

But when she walked out of the interview room, she met the officer from the lobby, hurrying her way.

"I was just coming to ask you if you could step outside for a moment," he said. "There are two people here who have asked to see you. They say it's in connection with this attempted crime."

"Can you take a phone to the interview room in the meantime, please?" Katie said. "The accused wants to get his lawyer here."

"I'll do that," the officer said.

Meanwhile, Katie hurried back to the lobby. There, she saw that two people were waiting. Both were men, and looked as if they could be brothers. Tall, rugged, with sandy blonde hair, and one was still wearing a race number on the front of his parka.

"I'm Agent Katie Winter," she said, walking over. "I understand you want to give some information on this attempted crime?"

The men exchanged a glance. "Yes," the one wearing the race number said. "I'm Mike Trident and this is my brother, Garth. We do want to tell you something in connection with this. Will it be kept confidential?"

"If it forms part of the case, we'll need to put it in the record. If it's just background or hearsay, there will be no need for that," Katie said, wondering what this was about, and whether this information would help to clear Taylor or bury him.

The brothers regarded one another dubiously. And then, Mike nodded.

"It's probably going to form part of the case. So I'm willing for it to go on the record."

"Thank you," Katie said. This was sounding like evidence against Taylor, and the more of that they could get now, the better. "Let's go somewhere private, and then you can tell me."

Feeling a flare of excitement as she headed down the corridor, she wondered what bombshell these men had come to deliver.

CHAPTER TWENTY FIVE

Katie walked down the corridor with her two witnesses until they were in a more private part of the police department. She decided that this would make it easier for Mike and Garth to tell her everything they knew.

It would have been nice to go into an actual office, but in this shoebox-sized police department, the only unoccupied room was a broom closet, so down the corridor would have to do.

She waited quietly for them to be ready to tell her what they'd come to say. They seemed very uneasy about it. Reluctant. That was good though. It told her that what they had to say was serious, and that it was going to have implications. They weren't taking this mission lightly. She could see they were conflicted about speaking to her.

Eventually, taking a deep breath, the blonde, weathered-looking Mike began, fixing Katie with a surprisingly intense, blue-eyed stare.

"We know this man, Matt Taylor. We've known him for a few years. We've met up at various events and trained together. This isn't easy to say."

He hesitated, grimacing.

Then Garth continued. "He's always had big issues with Jett. As in, serious personal issues. He's had his guns out for him, big time."

"Or rather, his knives. And I feel bad that we didn't say something before now, because we were close to him. We should have known and we should have warned somebody. Now, I feel like we're responsible for a big disaster by keeping quiet."

"What did you pick up?" Katie asked.

"He has said before now that he hates Jett, that he thinks he bought his way instead of trained his way to the top. Look, Jett has insulted him in the past, he's also lost his temper, so I mean, you could say there has been fault on both sides."

"But Jett was provoked," Garth added.

"True. Taylor always pushed him to the stage where he exploded, he had a knack for doing that. But when he was drunk, Taylor would always say that if Jett won a major race he was going to make sure he would be the ultimate loser. He used to say that he had a whole revenge planned, that it would be quick, and that he wouldn't hesitate."

"That he would be bold," Garth said.

"You have proof of this?" Katie asked softly.

"I actually do have a recording from a couple of months ago," Garth Trident said. "That's why we wanted to talk to you. It was recorded off our phone. I decided to capture some of it one night, when he was letting off steam to someone else at a bar, just in case - in case he ever did anything. Not that we ever thought he'd do something like that. This is horrific. I guess it was just in case."

"We didn't do enough, actually," Mike said.

Katie stared at them, feeling sympathetic.

"It's always easy to say that after the fact," she said. "But at least you're here now and you do have proof of what was threatened publicly. I am very glad you've come forward with this. It'll strengthen the case."

"We didn't want to be involved in a big fight that might affect the racing fraternity, but we had no idea this entire situation would turn into such a runaway train. I guess he was the one who's been killing here?"

"We are going to seek confirmation of that and look for the evidence," Katie said. "Were you aware of Taylor's movements in the past few days? Did you see any of his comings and goings?"

But to her disappointment, the brothers shook their heads.

"Unfortunately not. We were in a chalet all the way on the outskirts of the camping grounds, because we had dogs. He didn't participate in this race, though, that I do know. I think he said there were issues back home, that one of his dogs had been quarantined for something, so he couldn't travel with them. And he didn't stay in his usual place, with the other competitors. He stayed alone, in one of the small chalets on the far side, I think. I'm sure a lot of the racers had no idea he was here at all."

Quarantine sounded like a good excuse, Katie thought, for being at the festival and being able to move around freely, without the need to train and care for dogs.

All this information was coming in very handy to build a case for this having been preplanned.

"I just can't believe all this has happened, and we could maybe have stopped it," Garth said, looking stricken. "I guess we - we didn't realize until we saw him try to attack Jett."

"Nobody could have stopped it. You mustn't feel guilty about something you couldn't have known," Katie said. She knew only too well how an innocent, trusting member of the public might be reluctant to cause trouble, especially if they'd only overheard threats being made during drunken bragging at the bar.

"Well, we do feel bad. But we're here now, and that's about it. That's what we can say." Mike nodded apologetically.

"Thank you again. Please forward me the recording, and please ask any of the other racers to reach out if they have anything to say," she said.

"We'll do that."

Katie turned away, feeling glad that they had corroborating evidence that would help pull this case together, especially seeing their suspect was already lawyering up.

But as she turned away, treading back along the corridor, Katie had a very unwanted moment of self-doubt.

With every step she took, it seemed that misgivings were rushing in.

Would Taylor really have gone on a killing rampage if he'd been wanting to harm only one person? Why all the others? Why ensure that the entire festival was in a state of high alert, with police everywhere? It would have worked more in his favor to have kept a low profile and wait to carry out the kill.

Also, the Trident brothers had said he planned to take revenge if Jett won. But the other kills had played out before Jett's win, even though Katie knew he'd been a favorite to take first place. This was not as cut and dried as it seemed.

At that moment, Leblanc exited the interview room.

"Katie. You okay?" The anxiety on his face told her that he'd thought she'd been delayed because of a crisis with her sister. Quickly, she reassured him.

"I spoke to two racers who came forward to give testimony against Taylor. They've given a statement that he has previously threatened damage and harm to Jett, and stated that if Jett were ever to win a race, Taylor would make sure he lost straight afterward. They even sent a recording of the threats - it's a bit garbled, but it's clear."

120

Leblanc gave a grim, satisfied smile. "He's going down. For sure." Then he glanced at Katie's face.

"You don't think so?" he asked in surprise.

Katie sighed.

"I'm second guessing myself, I think. Wondering why he would have killed the others. Why not focus on his main target? Why alert people?"

Leblanc shook his head. "Because he's a violent psychopath. This was probably all part of his whole ego trip. Maybe Jett used them for various things and that made them into his targets. But logistically, was his time accounted for? Did they offer an alibi or confirm Taylor's whereabouts at the times of the killings?"

Leblanc spoke in his best 'cross examiner' tone and Katie knew he was strongly challenging her doubts, forcing her to reassess them.

"No. They said Taylor didn't bring dogs, he didn't compete, and hardly anyone knew he was here at all."

"Well, then. Let the evidence guide you," Leblanc said. "Don't let this idiot start making you second guess yourself. He's going down for murder, and attempted murder. Hopefully there'll be some trace left on that knife we've got in evidence now - which by the way, is extremely sharp."

Katie nodded. It was wrong to doubt herself and it could also affect her interrogation. She needed to push forward with confidence and intent as soon as Taylor's lawyer arrived.

But at that moment, there was a commotion from the interview room. Shouts of anger and protest resonated out into the corridor.

With her adrenaline spiking, Katie rushed back, Leblanc close behind. What was going on?

She burst into the interview room, to find the RCMP officer busy trying to calm down Taylor, whose composure had deserted him. He now looked angry, scared, and upset.

"He needs a new lawyer," the officer said breathlessly, retrieving the phone from the corner where Taylor had clearly thrown it with his one free hand.

"What's wrong with his existing lawyer?" Katie asked.

"My existing lawyer can't come out!" Taylor bellowed. "I just called his offices, and they told me he's deceased!"

With a thrill of horror, Katie listened to the words, thinking to herself that this changed everything, that there was no way this man could be such a good actor as to pretend he didn't know.

Shouting and ranting, Taylor continued. "Mr. Menzies has been my lawyer for years! He does all my work! I trust him! And his secretary just told me he died! That he was killed last night at the festival!"

CHAPTER TWENTY SIX

Taylor's words hit Katie like a slap across the face. Like a blast of a northern gale, chilling her spine. The man was speaking the truth. She saw it in his frantic body language, the sense of desperation that exuded from him. He wasn't lying. This was no clever bluff.

And that meant he hadn't known. Which in turn meant he wasn't the killer, which made her feel as if she was in freefall, plummeting down in a darkened elevator.

This was simply impossible.

Glancing at Leblanc, she saw the same frozen disbelief in his eyes.

"You were at the festival. Did you not know about this?" she interrogated him sternly.

"Know? How could I have known? I wasn't even there yesterday. I drove out to one of the observation posts along the way, to watch the long distance teams go by." His face darkened.

Katie was sure that if he was telling the truth, Taylor had done this for nefarious reasons. Maybe he'd been looking to check if Jett was in the lead so that he could plan his actions. But if he was telling the truth, it also meant he would not have known about any of the latest gossip and news, especially if he'd headed out solo.

"Did anyone see you out there?" she asked.

"I was on my own. I travel on my own. Why would I take people along? My motto in life is trust nobody," he seethed.

"And where have you been staying?"

"In the chalets, to the northwest of the site. They're the ones beyond the tree line that nobody wants because they're in the wind. So they're cheaper. Everywhere else is sheltered, which is like a miracle in this area. That there's anywhere with no wind, I mean. So I was staying there. On my own. Everyone else was racing. I couldn't bring my dogs because of the quarantine issue. I didn't fake that. Didn't pretend it. I wanted to race. But I couldn't."

"And the night before, what time were you here?"

"All day. Wandering around. Buying beers. Watching the dogs. Chilling out. I work hard. Work locally in town as a mechanic. This was my down time."

"Can anyone confirm that?"

He shook his head. "I probably said hi to a few, here and there. But I didn't keep track of the time."

"Did you know Thomas Briggs, the notary?"

"Never heard of him. Was he one of the guys who was murdered?"

"Yes he was. But he was from town. How come you didn't know him? Surely you know most people as a mechanic?"

"Two reasons. Either he didn't own a vehicle, or else he owned a newer one that was on a service plan and didn't need my help. Most cars on service plans, their owners take them south for maintenance, for as long as the maintenance contract lasts."

That made sense to Katie.

"Did you know Kevin, the other victim who was killed?"

He frowned. "I knew of him. He used to camp on this land, long ago. He owned a campervan. I fixed it up after he sold it. He sold it because the land was sold and he was asked to move off it, and the campervan wasn't in a condition back then to go far. I don't think he ever paid for staying there, but while it was in between owners, he lodged on it. But they had to move him; the deal couldn't go through while there were squatters. That's what they called him, a squatter, and I believe he tried to enforce his squatter's rights, and refused to move off the land for a while. It was almost as if he thought he owned it, and it was surprisingly difficult to get him to leave. Eventually, I think they did compensate him, give him some money to set him up afterward. I know that because my lawyer mentioned it to me and he was the one who organized that."

Even though he was rambling, Katie was listening. There was no such thing as useless information now, she decided.

"Kevin became like a gypsy. Like a traveler. He went around the country from place to place, living at events and roughing it in between. I heard of him. He was probably a good for nothing guy. But he didn't deserve to die. And if you think I was threatening Jett seriously, you're wrong. Of course I wasn't! You don't understand me at all. You probably think I'm lying about everything now."

Now he sounded as if he was speaking from the heart. "If Menzies was still alive, if he was here, he'd help me with this. I literally just wanted to scare him. I wanted to cut off his race number and tell him he didn't deserve it. That's what the knife was for. Yeah, I was angry. But going to kill him? In front of so many people? You think I'm dumb, don't you? Or that I have a death wish? Why would I do that? But now, I don't have anyone to represent me so I'm just telling you."

He sat taller in his chair.

"I hope you believe me now. I shouldn't need to convince you that I didn't kill anyone. I didn't hurt anyone. I'm innocent. I'm an innocent man."

Katie could see that the man was so distraught that he was about to burst into tears. He was genuinely upset and in a state of panic.

Katie thought his version was highly exaggerated. She wasn't buying that his actions had been so innocent.

But one thing was of interest to her, and that was that Kevin, the random drifter who'd had the stall at the festival, had previously been a camper on the site. In fact, he'd almost been in 'possession' of it at one stage, and had to move before the sale could go through.

Suddenly, there was a common theme. And Katie was starting to realize what it was.

It was the land itself. Not the festival. This was bigger than that. This wasn't about the festival but the venue.

That idyllic, large, perfectly situated area that was far more sheltered than the rest of this windswept town. The area that had become the venue, and that she remembered hearing that Pope had acquired the venue a few years ago in his attempts to expand the festival and make it a real draw card for the town. His brother had bought it and donated it to the town.

But even the environmentalist had mentioned that if there was a conflict, it would be over the land itself. That had been his first, instinctive reaction when Katie had asked him.

The answers had been there, like shadows in a dimly lit room, almost impossible to see until you knew they were there.

Now, she did know they were there but Katie still had no idea what they might mean.

She still didn't know who the killer was, but she was sure he must somehow be connected to the land.

Kevin had lived on the land. The notary would have helped in selling the land. The lawyer had helped evict Kevin.

Everyone who'd died was tied into it somehow. The killer had been working methodically through a list that made sense to him and now, also, made sense to Katie. She might not know who it was, but she knew that it was all connected. The land itself was the common denominator. And it had provided the motive for these killings.

"Thank you. I'll be back in a minute," she said to Taylor.

"But what about my lawyer?" Taylor shouted at them. He was still handcuffed. "I'm an innocent man! You have to give me my lawyer!"

Katie and Leblanc didn't say anything, choosing to ignore him as they strode out of the room.

Her mind was racing. This was so critically important. She was sure now that all the victims had died in the same place for a well-chosen reason, according to the killer's logic. On that land. At that one location.

"You can take him down to the cells for now," she said to the officer, glancing back at the room where Taylor was still shouting.

It was the location, not the festival.

Which meant the murders were all connected. All connected to the land. And now, she had two options open to her. The first was to go back in the records and find out who this person was. That would take time, and it might also be futile if the land had passed through a number of hands, or if the killer had not been an actual owner but had been an evicted resident or renter, similar to Kevin. Or perhaps even someone who had made an unsuccessful offer for it.

But it didn't matter who he was, because now, based on the pattern of what she had seen, Katie was sure that she knew who he would kill next.

She needed to hurry now, because she was sure the killer was just waiting until he could get that person alone.

CHAPTER TWENTY SEVEN

"I know who he's targeting next," Katie said to Leblanc, her voice tight and urgent, as soon as they were out of the police department and heading for the car.

"Who?" he asked, sounding anxious. "I wasn't following his logic. I was too busy looking for weak points in his version. What did you pick up?"

"I picked up that everyone who has been killed thus far has been strongly connected with the land. As in, pivotal in its changing hands."

"That's the logic?" Leblanc sounded thoughtful yet excited by this theory, as Katie strove to explain further.

"Look at all the people who were killed. Kevin squatted on it in a campervan, claimed squatter's rights, and had to be paid off to make him move. I didn't know that till now. The notary was killed and the town's lawyer who dealt with Kevin was killed. Someone has a real grudge over this land changing hands, and might have believed it was unfairly done or that they are in fact the rightful, entitled owner."

"So in that case, we might not know who the killer is, but we can predict the next target?"

"Exactly. And it'll be someone who not many people know about, but the killer knows because he's done his research. It'll be Pope's brother, Jason. The one who bought the land. The one who the killer believes got it unfairly. This is a revenge move, Leblanc, and Jason is now in serious danger. We have to find him!"

"Yes," Leblanc said, and Katie saw he was now fully on board with her theory. "At first, when I started thinking this way, I wondered if Pope might be targeted. But he's not the one involved with the land's ownership; he just runs the festival. We need to go and look for Jason, and get him to safety."

"Before the killer gets him," Katie said somberly.

As she climbed into the car, Leblanc was already on the phone, calling Pope.

"Hello?" Pope answered sounding bright and cheerful, the voice of a man who thought the danger was past and that everything was back on track.

"We've got a problem," Leblanc said. "We are fairly sure the man in custody is not the killer."

"What?" Pope said. "But - but why? What makes you think that? You were so sure. I was sure. He attacked Jett with a knife!"

"We'll go into the details later," Leblanc said. "For now, though, we need to ask you - where's Jason?"

There was a short, shocked silence.

"Jason? Why?"

"He's the killer's next target," Leblanc said. "We need to get him to safety. Now."

Katie honked at a slow moving car in her way and swerved around it, trying to get to the festival grounds faster as she sped along the icy road.

"That can't be true," Pope said, as if repeating it to himself would make it sound any less absurd. "Jason hasn't even been involved in the festival. He's been visiting here today. He went for a sled ride, had some food, spoke to a few people. He's been enjoying it along with everyone else. That's all."

She could see that Pope was still trying to process this information. But his voice was sounding scared and shaky. Katie could tell his brother meant the world, and that this was a horrible shock.

"The land is the common denominator. Not the festival. The killer is targeting all the people who were involved in swapping the recent land ownership. He has a grudge against this happening, and he's been targeting everyone who was involved in making that deal."

"I don't understand," Pope said disbelievingly.

"The land's the key. Everything's connected to the land. It's the motive."

"But..." Pope's voice sounded hollow.

"We can explain later. For now, finding Jason is the most important step. Can you call him?"

Now, Pope's breathing sounded rapid.

"Call him? Sure I - I can. I'm here near the podium, doing some photos. Let me try call him on my other phone. Will you wait?"

"Sure," Leblanc said, as Katie sped along the road. They were almost back at the festival now and it was busier than ever, she noted, feeling frustrated that the press of crowds would make it harder to find him.

"I'm calling him," Pope said. "He hasn't answered yet. Let me keep trying. It might be too noisy where he is."

"Do you have any idea where he might be?"

"He might be down at the finish line watching the sprint races. And I know he was going to go to the temporary race office on site after that, to try and fix a printer that was acting up. Perhaps that's it. Perhaps he's busy with the printer now."

Now Pope sounded absolutely terrified at what the alternative reason might be for his brother not picking up.

"What's he wearing?"

"He's wearing a white jacket. And a red knit cap. That's what I remember anyway. I hope I'm not wrong about that. What if I'm wrong?" Pope sounded breathless with consternation.

"We're here now," Katie said, pulling to a stop in the crowded parking lot and yanking the car door open. "We've just arrived. We're going to search for him, and brief all the cops to do the same. Keep trying to get ahold of him and you are also welcome to look for him but - but take a cop with you," she warned. "Don't go alone."

Then she cut the call. It was time to search the festival for the killer's next victim - a man who loved the town and who definitely did not deserve to die at his hands.

"We need to go separate ways," Katie said to Leblanc. She didn't want to do this. It would be much safer to stay together, but the danger to them was not as great as the certain danger to Jason. With every moment now vitally important, the more ground they could cover, the better.

"I'll go and look by the finish of the sprint races," Leblanc said. "And on my way, I'll brief the cops also."

"I'll go and find the temporary office," Katie said. "Maybe he's near there, or they will know where he went."

But she had a cold feeling in her stomach as she set off at a run, following the signs to the office, treading over the packed snow, weaving through the throngs of spectators that were enjoying the early afternoon fun.

There was a family atmosphere here. The laughter, the cheers, the happy sound of the crowd, the vendors laughing, and the musicians

129

playing their music. And yet, in the midst of it, there was an imminent threat that had never been more serious or more intense.

She hurried along, looking out for the office. She jogged past groups of people who were laughing and having fun, enjoying the party atmosphere, watching the fun and games, without a care in the world. Clearly they didn't think they were in danger, and they weren't. Only one person was, and it might be too late for him.

The unanswered phone was a very bad sign. She didn't want to think too hard about it, because there might be an innocent reason, but deep in her heart, Katie feared that the killer might already have grabbed Jason.

But even if he had, there was surely still a chance of saving his life, if they could find which way he'd gone. At least, before the killer delivered the final slash to the neck. So far, with the other victims, he'd moved them first. The kill had been the next move. Perhaps that gave them time.

At that moment. Katie saw what she was looking for. It was a small wooden cabin, on the outskirts of the festival area, with a discreet notice outside: Race Office.

She imprinted the memory of Jason's face, and the clothing he was wearing, in her mind again.

Feeling hopeful that he would either be inside, or else they would know where he'd gone, Katie rushed over to the door.

CHAPTER TWENTY EIGHT

"Jason Pope. Is he here somewhere, or do you know where he has gone?" Katie asked breathlessly, bursting into the door of the small on-site organizer's office.

The woman behind the desk looked up inquiringly. From behind her, a fan heater rattled loudly in the small space that smelled of pine boards.

"Jason was here. He was fixing the printer. Where did he go? Let me think. I don't remember him saying. Have you tried to call him?"

"He's not picking up," Katie said. "We think he might be in danger. I need to find him."

The woman looked concerned. "I can't say. I think someone needed him and he headed out. But I don't know where he went, and I didn't see who it was. Unfortunately I was on the phone at the time. It's been very busy here this morning. We've had more calls than usual as a result of all this trouble. People have been calling and asking if it'll be safe. We heard an arrest had been made, so I have been telling them it is safe now," she said, looking at them anxiously.

"Did Jason give you any clues? Maybe mention a name, or a specific location?" Katie asked, desperately trying to jog the woman's memory in case she had heard something important.

At that moment, a blast of music from outside boomed around the showgrounds, drowning out her next words. With her hands theatrically over her ears, she grimaced apologetically at Katie.

"The live band's started. From here it gets quite loud," she shouted. "I don't remember anything. He just spoke and went out!"

Loud was an understatement. Deafening was more the word Katie would have used. The music that was now resounding through the area was going to make their job ten times more difficult. There was no way Jason could answer his phone now.

Katie walked out despondently, feeling the air throbbing with the bass notes of the band that were being relayed around the grounds via giant speakers.

She noticed for the first time that there was a laminated map of the festival grounds attached to the side of the wall, similar to the one she'd seen outside the main offices when she first arrived, but this one even bigger and more intricate. Glancing at it, she wondered if it would give her any insight as to where he'd gone.

It was a detailed map, with topography and trees, hills and rivers shown, as well as the main areas where the festival was taking place - the dog training grounds, the campsite, the kiosks, the accommodations. Looking at the map, Katie wondered for the first time - if this land was so highly significant to the killer, was it possible that he'd chosen each of the locations with a purpose in mind?

Could that be why he'd chosen to kill the first victim near the dog training camp, the second victim near the kiosks, and the third victim in the vicinity of the southern campsite and chalets?

Was it a different area for each kill?

Or was it not anything to do with the festival, Katie suddenly wondered, looking at where north was on the map. Perhaps the areas were just coincidental, and what she should be focusing on was the geographical coordinates, to see if there was any pattern there.

After all, the festival itself was not what was important to this killer. That, she'd figured out. It was the land that was of great significance.

So, was there a reason for why these victims had been taken to these locations?

She didn't have exact coordinates where each of the bodies had been found, but she did have a memory in her head of more or less where they were located.

Frowning, with the tip of her finger, she traced the approximate areas on the map.

The area where they'd first walked, with Aaron the dog musher, to see the first site - that had been here. Katie pointed to the area, noticing that it was right on the eastern border of the demarcated land. Due east, she guessed.

Now that was interesting.

Where had Kevin's body been found? She thought back, trying to remember. Hikers had stumbled over it and it had been near the kiosks. That would have been on the far west side. Due west, in fact. That was where the kiosks were located.

Katie was starting to get excited. A theory was beginning to come together in her mind.

The third body, Menzies. Where had that been dumped? It had been close to where she went for her walk.

Due south!

A shiver went down her spine. This was getting more and more interesting.

She had found a pattern. The three bodies had been dumped in very specific and accurate locations, one due east of the grounds, one due west, and the third due south.

Katie's heart thudded.

They had been chosen with care. She was sure of it. And in this order. There was an extreme significance to his pattern.

Precision was the answer. He was an organized killer. A meticulous killer. And now that she had the pattern, Katie saw without a doubt where the next victim would be.

Jason Pope would be killed due north, on the fourth and final compass point of this beautiful and unique piece of land, the sale of which had triggered someone to commit these murders.

Due north. It was the thick forest. The deeply wooded border, that provided the shield from the wind and the worst of the weather.

Here. This area, where a tiny river crossed through the thick pine woods - that seemed to be the point that was precisely due north. Katie stared at the map, trying to imprint it on her mind. Then she photographed it with her phone.

Katie got on the phone, her heart racing, trying to get ahold of Leblanc. But he wasn't picking up. With the music so loud - and Katie guessed even louder where he was near the finish line, he most likely could not hear her. And there was no time to go and get him. If Jason Pope had disappeared, he could already have been taken.

But Katie knew her last hope rested on the fact that this killer seemed to think of his murders, in a way, as sacrifices. He only murdered the victims once their unconscious bodies were placed where he wanted them. Only then did he deliver that bold and merciless slash to the throat.

It might have taken him some time to lure Jason away - because that was now what she was sure had happened - to knock him out, and to take him to the exact spot that he'd earmarked for him, the place where he was going to let him bleed out in the snow, in his final, twisted, and ultimately meaningless revenge.

Quickly, she sent the map to Leblanc, with a short message about where she was going.

For now, she was on her own. It was up to her to save Jason's life.

If she could get there fast enough.

CHAPTER TWENTY NINE

With the map coordinates in her mind, Katie raced across the festival grounds, heart hammering. She bypassed the crowds, her feet thudding in time to the beat of the music, and pounded up the hill. She was heading due north. She had a picture in her mind of where to go, and exactly where in that dense, forested area the stream traversed the woods.

That was where he would be, the killer who was still unknown, but who was targeting a victim that she did know.

Jason Pope. Would she be in time to save the likeable landowner?

Looking from side to side as she ran, Katie hoped to see one or more of the RCMP officers. Backup now would be good, but she didn't have time to waste going to look. She guessed they were all clustered in the areas where people were. The northern border was quieter now. The killer had chosen the timing well.

She might be too late. If they'd only realized the significance of the land earlier, and plotted the kills.

Her breath burned in her lungs as she raced across the grounds, gradually leaving the music behind - although it was still loud, some of the sound was now absorbed and muffled by the silence of the woods ahead.

But there was another noise now, one she could hear faintly. The low, rumbling engine of a diesel pickup. He was there! This was about to happen. Katie felt her stomach twist as she sped up, running at full speed. Glancing back, she saw that a curve of the hill now hid her from view of the main site. Nobody could see her. Nobody could follow. She was on her own, racing against the killer's agenda as Jason's time ticked down.

There was the truck, ahead, a gray vehicle, dusty and dented, nondescript, parked in the shadow of the trees. It was empty, but its engine was still idling. A sign, perhaps, that the killer was going to make a quick getaway.

Katie slowed, gasping for breath, slipping on the chunky ice as she approached. This was his vehicle, he was here, and he must have brought Jason. But where were they?

Panic surged inside her at the thought she was too late, and Jason was already dead, covered in that thin layer of snow like the others, so that all she'd be able to do was stumble over him. She couldn't see any footprints in the chunky mess of ice and pine needles that was strewn over the forest floor.

And then, Katie remembered about the river, that little, narrow stream. That was where she could be, but where in the thick trees was her landmark?

At this time of year it would be iced over, maybe filled in with snow. But the banks might be visible. Its path through the trees could be traceable to a trained eye, and once long ago, Katie had possessed a trained eye that knew the forest well.

Drawing on old memories from a childhood spent in the woods, Katie breathed in, moving quietly forward, scanning the trees and the ground, looking for the signs that would tell her it was there.

She remembered the long days, the snowy winter mornings, the cries of laughter as she and Josie explored, dared, and adventured together, and felt her eyes burn in sadness. But that inherent knowledge had not left her, and now her subconscious did its work, piecing together the subtle geographical clues.

There it was. Over there, to the right. Thanks to her memory and instincts, she had found the almost invisible channel, wending its way through the trees. Gasping in another gulp of air, Katie set off toward it at a run.

And there he was. She saw him, with a lurch of her heart. He was in the channel, invisible to the passing eye unless you knew where to look and where to go. A tall man in a gray coat that was almost perfectly camouflaged against the background.

But the knife he had in his hand was easier to see, and Katie could clearly make out the dull gleam of steel as he raised it over the figure lying prone in front of him.

"Wait!" she screamed.

There wasn't time for more. Wasn't time for anything. There wasn't a clear line of sight to use her gun, or any guarantee that a bullet would stop him in time.

Katie raced for the trench and leaped down, her arms outstretched, hoping that her flying tackle would deflect the killing blow, and save this man's final victim.

She felt a jarring impact as she crashed into the icy trench, grabbing for his knife arm, trying to tug the killer off balance. Briefly, she saw Jason, collapsed in the trench, with a bloodied wound on his temple. She hoped he was still alive, because all her focus was on trying to fight his would-be killer. The man in the coat. The man with the knife.

He gave an outraged yell and staggered back, and then they were in hand to hand combat.

Katie had no doubt at all that this man was fighting for everything he had - and most importantly, for the chance to make the kill. And as for her, she found herself fighting to stay alive.

This man was furiously strong. He turned, snarling, his pale face drawn in a mask of rage. He slashed at her, and Katie ducked sideways, feeling cold with fear, because he had no inhibitions at all about using that knife. It was so much a part of him that she guessed he had experience - a farmer, a butcher. He'd sliced, skinned, cut, and diced. Whoever he was, she knew this without a doubt. And now, this lethal blade was flashing in her direction and she had to leap out of the way, her ankle twisting agonizingly and her boot soles slipping on the rough, icy surface.

"You can't stop me," he muttered, on the attack again, so that Katie had to jump back. "Nobody can stop me!" The eyes that met hers were feverish and bloodshot, and cold as ice. He had the advantage of height and reach, and he was thrashing and slashing with the knife.

He was utterly insane. Utterly focused on his goal.

She had the sense that, in a businesslike way, he was simply trying to dispatch her as quickly and efficiently as possible, before getting back to the mission he was busy with. She needed to get her gun out, but it was impossible, because this combat in the narrow, icy trench was now at close quarters and there was no time for anything but trying to survive.

Digging her feet into the slippery snow for purchase, Katie tried to grab his knife-wielding arm, but he evaded her attack. His eyes gleamed in triumph, as though he knew this was all too easy, that he was bound to win and that nothing she could do would stop him.

He stabbed down, and she scrabbled back, trying to get away, but he was reaching for her again. She wasn't going to let that happen. She took the escape route, diving sideways and away from the blade. She crashed against the side of the trench, snow and ice scattering around her.

She saw the glitter of the steel, sharp and deadly, and dived away, feeling the slash of the blade as it grazed her shoulder, ripping the fabric apart. She heard the tearing sound, but she didn't feel the cold, burning sting that would mean she had been cut. She'd escaped the edge of his blade - just. But it came at a cost. She skidded, lost her footing, and fell, landing heavily on her back.

She heard his breath hiss out in triumph.

Katie knew she had to get the offensive here; he had the advantage in every way, and this could mean the end for her.

She was exactly where he wanted her - and she had to change the odds.

There was only one thing she could do in the split second she had available.

Katie made a desperate grab with her gloved hand, grasping a palm-sized chunk of ice. As hard as she could, she flung it at him, hoping for an accurate shot, and that the sudden, surprising movement from her would slow him or distract him – at least for enough time for her to get to her feet.

The ice hit him on the cheek, a hard, accurate shot. He ducked, with a cry.

And then, Katie was up, grabbing for the knife arm with both her hands, knowing that against such a vicious fighter, this was her last chance to wrestle it out of his grasp.

CHAPTER THIRTY

Katie launched herself at this killer, knowing that she had only a moment before he recovered from the accurate blow. Again, she was shocked by how fast he was, how agile, and how strong.

She knew she had to disarm him and stop the murderous attack, but her plans, her efforts, had not been enough. She had to break his grip on the weapon.

Katie got a grasp on his wrist and tried to twist his hand, but he was clutching the knife too hard. She was going to need more than force to distract him; the chunk of ice hadn't been enough. His arm was like a steel bar, and he was bringing it inexorably toward her, using his strength against her, and for all her FBI training, Katie knew, strength was ultimately the deciding factor.

She tried every trick in the book she could think of. She stamped for his feet. She tried again to kick out at his knees but he was ready for her and he simply moved away, before aiming a brutal kick at her own knee which she only just avoided.

She was hanging onto his knife hand with all her strength, but her muscles were burning, and soon her arm would tire. Then, swiftly, he would destroy her.

What could she do?

The FBI had not only taught her physical techniques, as she felt her grip start to loosen, but they had taught her mental agility as well. And maybe now, in this icy ravine, losing the struggle, she should stop fighting this killer with her body and she should start using her mind.

And there was one key point she could use. One weak point, just one chance she had. She knew it because she had finally tuned into his logic and understood his reasons.

His mission, his reason for doing these kills, was to spill blood in four precisely calculated coordinates. That was his way of getting revenge for what he saw as the 'theft' of land that now belonged to all.

Katie, in the midst of her exhaustion and struggle, saw that she could use this to her advantage. And she realized exactly how.

She made her eyes focus on a point just beyond this man's big bulky shoulder. As if she was making eye contact with someone who had just woken up after being knocked out.

And she yelled, at the top of her voice, "Hey, Jason! Run! As fast as you can! Just get away! Climb out and get away from here!"

For a moment, she felt the man freeze. She saw the surprise on his face. The disbelief.

And then, she saw him realize what it would mean if Jason escaped. That he would lose his kill. Lose the last of the four murders that he needed. He would lose his location and wouldn't be able to spill the blood where he felt it had to be done.

His face changed. He tensed. Most definitely, Katie knew, he did not want his final victim to run away.

And he glanced around.

She was ready for that momentary lapse in focus.

As his head turned, she let go of his arm and swung the heel of her hand into his jaw with all the force she had.

She felt, as she struck him, that this was it, and she could do no more. But it was enough. She heard his teeth clack together and his head was knocked back. Stumbling, his momentum took him, reeling off balance, and he fell, sprawling on the ground with a cry.

With a last effort, she grabbed his hand, the one holding the knife. She got to his wrist, grabbed it with both hands, and summoning all the power she had, twisted it until she heard the man cry out again. It dropped from his fingers and she flung it away.

Then she kicked him in the head, and he went down.

She didn't know for how long he would be out. She guessed he was only temporarily stunned. If he revived now and got up again, there was nothing she could do. Nothing. She was completely spent.

Katie staggered away from him, dragging in ragged breaths of air. She felt her legs wobbling under her, and she slumped down, gasping. She had to stop and rest. There was no way she could walk another step; she was too exhausted to move. She could fight no more because this battle had drained her completely.

She hissed in a breath as she saw his legs start to move, his hands reaching out, groping. He was coming around, far faster than she'd thought. Somehow, this fight was going to have to continue. But Katie knew that this time, this strong and brutal man wouldn't just have the edge, but would be the winner. She had to get her gun out. In time.

Wrestling with her glove, she tried to pull it off so she could get to her holster, but her hand was shaking so violently that even this was difficult to do.

And then, from the edge of the woods, she heard a shout.

"Katie!"

It was Leblanc's voice.

"Katie! Are you there?"

Scrambling shakily to her knees, Katie tried to shout back, as loudly as she possibly could.

"I'm down here! Here. Come quick. He's out, but he's coming around. And we need a medevac. For Jason."

The thundering of multiple pairs of footsteps, as Leblanc and the RCMP headed in her direction, was the most welcome sound that Katie thought she had ever heard in her life.

*

Two hours later, she was sitting in the police department's back room, gulping down a welcome mug of hot chocolate, feeling safe and warm and utterly relieved.

The festival was still continuing. Bursts of colorful light from out the window told her that a silent fireworks display - out of respect to the animals - was under way. Strains of music also came in their direction, wafted by the wind. A few snowflakes were starting to fall and she guessed that by nightfall, it would be snowing heavily.

In the meantime, the visitors, the racers, and the town were celebrating. A triple victory, she thought. The festival had been saved. The owner of the land, Jason Pope, was already sitting up and talking in hospital, seeming well and healthy after his knock to the head.

And the killer was in police custody, locked in a cell, never to be a free man again.

Now, Katie knew his name was Adrian Grover. He was the son of one of the land's previous owners, a man who'd defaulted on his payments after purchasing a fragment of the property. Adrian's father had ended up in jail himself, a hardened alcoholic who had killed another man during a bar fight. Adrian, thanks partly to inheriting these violent tendencies and partly, Katie was sure, to a violent and abusive upbringing, was a hardened psychopath. He worked part-time in a slaughterhouse, which is where Katie guessed he'd learned his knife skills.

She guessed that the communication with his father in jail had reinforced in both of their minds that the land was rightfully theirs and had been unfairly taken away. Perhaps it had been his father's death, late last year, that had finally triggered Adrian to start on the revenge killings.

But he would kill no more, and Soaring Crow was safe.

Katie looked up and saw to her surprise that Pope had arrived. The festival organizer was standing at the back office door with an RCMP officer who'd escorted him through. His hands were jammed into the pockets of his coat, and he had a rueful smile on his face.

"Katie," he said. "I'm glad I caught you before you left. I wanted to thank you. What you did was amazing. You saved my brother. That means everything to me. And you saved the festival. I was fighting so hard for it to survive, that I was refusing to see how close we came to jeopardizing it totally. I'm sorry I spoke against you and opposed what you wanted to do."

"I appreciate your passion for the town," Katie smiled. "And I'm so relieved that Jason will be okay. You are two really good men. I wish every town had more people like you."

"And the same goes for the both of you," Pope said, and to her surprise he stepped forward and gave both her and Leblanc a warm, genuine, bear hug.

And then, the sound of chopper blades was suddenly audible outside, and Katie stood up, as did Leblanc, quickly gathering their things.

They said a warm goodbye to the local RCMP officers, and then hurried outside into the dusky, snowy, late afternoon.

Scott had organized the helicopter so that they could both return as speedily as possible. It was going to do a special stop for her first, at Rochester General Hospital.

Katie was grateful.

Because Josie's medical team was meeting with her parents in the evening, and they had an urgent decision to make.

CHAPTER THIRTY ONE

By the time Katie walked into the hospital that night, she felt like a nervous wreck.

After a stunning conclusion to the case, and a feeling of triumph and relief, the afternoon had gone sharply downhill.

Firstly, to her consternation, Leblanc had spent the chopper ride back messaging someone on his phone. Katie hadn't wanted to ask him about it. She hadn't felt as if she was entitled to ask. She had been the one who had called off the romance with him and who had said a firm no when he'd gently asked her to reconsider.

But even though he'd tried to do it discreetly, Katie had seen how he behaved and how he looked as he had sent those texts. She'd seen the incline of his head, the quirk of his lips. She had absolutely no doubt that these were flirtatious texts. If he was not dating someone, he was thinking about doing it. He was getting emotionally involved. He'd met someone else.

And knowing that hurt Katie so badly that she felt like recklessly rewinding her life and rethinking every decision, from the time she'd pulled away from getting close and told Leblanc she wasn't ready.

Maybe she hadn't felt ready.

But then again, maybe she hadn't really known that she was ready, and now it was too late, and she felt curdled with worry inside as she fretted that this was yet another bad life decision she'd made that would come back to haunt her. She couldn't bear to think of what this would involve, how Leblanc would start mentioning this new lover, how he'd care for her, how Katie might even one day meet the woman who he'd fallen for, after Leblanc had tried and failed with her.

She recoiled from this. She felt shattered, she felt envious, and above all, the voices of self-recrimination were loud and accusing. This was her fault. What else had she thought would happen? Leblanc wasn't going to live the life of a monk for all eternity because Katie had rejected him!

Even if that monastic existence was all she thought she deserved or was ready for herself, she knew that Leblanc was a loving and passionate man, every inch a romantic Frenchman, and for him, love was part of life.

It could have been that way for her too, and now Katie was starting to think that it should have been. She'd blown it.

By the time the chopper landed, Katie felt sick. She'd bidden Leblanc only the briefest goodbye, unable to make eye contact with him. Jumping out of the chopper, she'd hustled into the hospital.

She was heading for the elevator, when she realized she was on a collision course with another woman.

Quickly, Katie stepped back, muttering an apology to the tall, slender woman with bushy gray hair and a strong, weathered face that she'd nearly smashed right into.

"Sorry," she said, and quickly made to step past her, still buried in her own worries, her own world, not even glancing at the other woman.

But she realized to her surprise that the other woman wasn't moving.

She was standing in place and staring at Katie with a strange expression.

"Our meeting was not unintentional, Ms. Winter," she said, in a low voice that was surprisingly melodious. "I've been looking for you."

Blinking, Katie took a step back and stared at her.

"I'm sorry. What do you mean? Who are you?"

She realized it sounded rude, but she was short on patience and at that moment, all out of tact.

"I'm Honore Eliot. I've just been visiting a patient at the hospital and was on my way out when I saw you arrive. I know who you are. I've seen you and your parents here before, even though you have probably not noticed me."

"You have?" Katie said.

Despite her inner anguish, and the fact she was anxious to get this meeting over with, there was something strangely soothing about this woman's voice. Oddly, Katie felt as if flickers of angst inside her were being calmed. There was a brightness in her wise, dark eyes.

"Your sister's predicament is very sad. People have been talking about it. Everyone who comes to this hospital regularly knows about it."

"So you visit here regularly?"

144

"I do. And because of that, I wanted to make you a suggestion. An offer."

"What's that?"

Katie stared into Honore's dark eyes, without the faintest clue what she might be going to say. She didn't even know who she was or how she fit into the picture. Perhaps seeing her confusion, Honore continued.

"I am a hypnotist by profession. A very skilled one."

"A hypnotist?" Katie repeated incredulously.

"I work throughout New York State. Much of my work in hospitals involves pain management, and the speeding up of healing, but I also specialize in psychiatric cases. In unlocking memories."

Katie stared at her, feeling shivers cascade up and down her spine.

Unlocking memories? That was exactly what they feared the problem with Josie was. That she was imprisoned in her mind, in her past, in where she'd been captured for so many years.

"And you can help with Josie?" Katie asked incredulously. "You really think so?"

"I feel sure I can. I have a good success rate. There are risks involved, I must be truthful with you about that, but generally they are minor, and the improvements far outweigh them."

Katie wanted to ask more about these risks, but Honore was already continuing. "You are welcome to look on my website and read about a few of the cases I've worked with. I can see the pain you and your family are in. I feel for your sister. Being trapped in your own mind is the worst kind of imprisonment. There's no easy escape from it. I would like to try and help you."

Honore handed her a business card.

Katie took it wordlessly, feeling utterly shocked by this surprise offer.

"Think about it," Honore said. "Call me. My phone is open any time of the day or night to talk. I truly believe that this can only help, especially in your sister's situation. It might be the key to her healing." Her eyes held Katie's for a long moment. "At the very least, it will be an option to try, before you seek more permanent solutions from which there might be no return."

Without a doubt, Katie knew that the entire hospital had been talking about this. Most probably the nurses on the team had discussed Josie's decline with others, and word had spread. At any rate, Honore was hinting strongly that she knew about the upcoming decision and that ECT was in the cards for Josie.

"Thank you. I appreciate this. I'll discuss it and be in touch soon," Katie said shortly, even though there was a lot more she knew she could say, and more she wanted to ask, too. She was simply too shocked to be able to get any more words out.

With a grave nod, Honore turned and walked away, and Katie headed for the elevator, feeling stunned.

She had never thought there would be such an option. And now, at the last moment, Honore was saying this might work?

Surely it couldn't hurt, she thought. Surely it might be worth a try?

She had no idea what her parents or the doctors would say, but Katie thought that this might be a viable option, a last ditch attempt at a less invasive therapy before the ECT from which there would be no going back.

And at least, this hypnosis surely could not leave Josie worse than before.

Or could it, Katie wondered with a shudder, realizing how little she knew about what was really going on in her sister's scarred and damaged mind.

She was going to tell her parents and the doctors at this meeting, she decided. She was going to say that she wanted to go ahead with this. And if they didn't agree, she was going to do her damnedest to persuade them. It truly felt like their last hope for healing her, the one avenue they hadn't yet explored at all.

If there was a chance of unlocking her sister's memories and exhuming the dark demons of fear and trauma that had infiltrated her mind, then Katie knew she had to try. Even though she was scared to think what those memories would be, and what terrible truths she might have to face if they saw the light of day.

WATCH ME
(A Katie Winter FBI Suspense Thriller—Book 11)

The warm weather brings brief but welcome relief to the unforgiving Canadian terrain—but with the melting of the snow comes a horrifying discovery. FBI Special Agent Katie Winter follows the killer down a dark and dangerous path—but can she solve the case before it swallows her whole?

"Molly Black has written a taut thriller that will keep you on the edge of your seat… I absolutely loved this book and can't wait to read the next book in the series!"
—Reader review for Girl One: Murder

WATCH ME is book #11 in a new series by #1 bestselling mystery and suspense author Molly Black.

FBI Special Agent Katie Winter is no stranger to frigid winters, isolation, and dangerous cases. With her sterling record of hunting down serial killers, she is a fast-rising star in the BAU, and Katie is the natural choice to partner with Canadian law enforcement to track killers across brutal and unforgiving landscapes.

A page-turning and harrowing crime thriller featuring a brilliant and tortured FBI agent, the KATIE WINTER series is a riveting mystery, packed with non-stop action, suspense, twists and turns, revelations, and driven by a breakneck pace that will keep you flipping pages late into the night. Fans of Rachel Caine, Teresa Driscoll and Robert Dugoni are sure to fall in love.

Future books in the series will be available soon!

"I binge read this book. It hooked me in and didn't stop till the last few pages… I look forward to reading more!"
—Reader review for Found You

"I loved this book! Fast-paced plot, great characters and interesting insights into investigating cold cases. I can't wait to read the next book!"

—Reader review for Girl One: Murder

"Very good book... You will feel like you are right there looking for the kidnapper! I know I will be reading more in this series!"
—Reader review for Girl One: Murder

"This is a very well written book and holds your interest from page 1... Definitely looking forward to reading the next one in the series, and hopefully others as well!"
—Reader review for Girl One: Murder

"Wow, I cannot wait for the next in this series. Starts with a bang and just keeps going."
—Reader review for Girl One: Murder

"Well written book with a great plot, one that will keep you up at night. A page turner!"
—Reader review for Girl One: Murder

"A great suspense that keeps you reading... can't wait for the next in this series!"
—Reader review for Found You

"Sooo soo good! There are a few unforeseen twists... I binge read this like I binge watch Netflix. It just sucks you in."
—Reader review for Found You

Molly Black

Bestselling author Molly Black is author of the MAYA GRAY FBI suspense thriller series, comprising nine books (and counting); of the RYLIE WOLF FBI suspense thriller series, comprising six books (and counting); of the TAYLOR SAGE FBI suspense thriller series, comprising eight books (and counting); of the KATIE WINTER FBI suspense thriller series, comprising eleven books (and counting); and of the RUBY HUNTER FBI suspense thriller series, comprising three books (and counting).

An avid reader and lifelong fan of the mystery and thriller genres, Molly loves to hear from you, so please feel free to visit www.mollyblackauthor.com to learn more and stay in touch.

BOOKS BY MOLLY BLACK

MAYA GRAY MYSTERY SERIES
GIRL ONE: MURDER (Book #1)
GIRL TWO: TAKEN (Book #2)
GIRL THREE: TRAPPED (Book #3)
GIRL FOUR: LURED (Book #4)
GIRL FIVE: BOUND (Book #5)
GIRL SIX: FORSAKEN (Book #6)
GIRL SEVEN: CRAVED (Book #7)
GIRL EIGHT: HUNTED (Book #8)
GIRL NINE: GONE (Book #9)

RYLIE WOLF FBI SUSPENSE THRILLER
FOUND YOU (Book #1)
CAUGHT YOU (Book #2)
SEE YOU (Book #3)
WANT YOU (Book #4)
TAKE YOU (Book #5)
DARE YOU (Book #6)

TAYLOR SAGE FBI SUSPENSE THRILLER
DON'T LOOK (Book #1)
DON'T BREATHE (Book #2)
DON'T RUN (Book #3)
DON'T FLINCH (Book #4)
DON'T REMEMBER (Book #5)
DON'T TELL (Book #6)
DON'T HIDE (Book #7)
DON'T BLINK (Book #8)

KATIE WINTER FBI SUSPENSE THRILLER
SAVE ME (Book #1)
REACH ME (Book #2)
HIDE ME (Book #3)
BELIEVE ME (Book #4)
HELP ME (Book #5)

FORGET ME (Book #6)
HOLD ME (Book #7)
PROTECT ME (Book #8)
REMEMBER ME (Book #9)
CATCH ME (Book #10)
WATCH ME (Book #11)

RUBY HUNTER FBI SUSPENSE THRILLER
IF I RUN (Book #1)
IF I TELL (Book #2)
IF I LIVE (Book #3)

Made in United States
North Haven, CT
14 February 2025

65820370R00093